Dance With a Tornado

and other short stories

J.L. Fredrick

To the Lopez family —
Enjoy!
J.L. Fredrick
"Joel"
7/27/2014

Allow imagination to break the barriers,

and brush up against yesterday.

—J.L. Fredrick—

J.L. FREDRICK

Contents

Dance

With a

Tornado

and other

short stories

DANCE

WITH

A

TORNADO

J.L. FREDRICK

DANCE WITH A TORNADO
J.L. Fredrick

1.

The gas gauge read a little more than half full. Casey figured he would be somewhere in Iowa by the time he needed gas, and by then he'd probably be tired enough to stop for a little sleep, too. He'd been staring into the sun hovering over the western horizon for a while now, and it wouldn't be long until dusk would provide a little relief.

Casey Lane was anxious to see his friend again. Larry's father had been transferred to Colorado Springs last summer, just after the boys' high school graduation, and their only contact since had been occasionally by cell phone.

The miles sailed past his open car window as Casey gave some thought to the fact that he didn't have any idea what he would do in Colorado. In reality, he had no idea what he wanted to do with the rest of his life. His father would help him financially through college, but at nineteen, he was still quite confused about where his interests pointed him. This cloud of disorder led him to believe he should see the world—or at least some of it—before making any decisions about settling down into a career. How could he be expected to choose an option if he didn't know what the options were? So he would start with Colorado, and a brief look at what lay between it and his home state of Michigan.

A slight vibration that he had noticed in the car earlier was now accompanied by a vivid rattling noise, more apparent with every mile. Casey was no expert mechanic, but he knew enough about cars to understand that the noise was the product of a potentially serious mechanical malfunction. He needed to stop soon.

His father had warned him about the probability of a breakdown with his old car on a cross-country trip. His father had warned him about a lot of things, and Casey realized that he'd probably been right about most of them, including his 1982 Oldsmobile Cutlass with well over a hundred thousand miles on the odometer. Regardless of the advice, here he was, in southwestern Wisconsin and a thousand miles from his destination with a failing car.

He let the car coast in neutral up the Ripley exit ramp. The noise was much quieter and the vibration less, but as soon as he shifted back to drive and turned left toward what appeared to be a truck stop, the noise and vibration returned with even more intensity. Casey wished this wasn't happening; just once he wanted to show his father that he could make a decision and do something on his own that turned out okay. Apparently this was not it.

Casey just sat in the car staring out the windshield at the back wall of the truck stop store where he parked. If he called his father, he'd have to listen to the I-told-you-so speech. It would be another humiliating incident burned into his memory, along with all the other memories of his father reminding him of mistakes and bad decisions. Not that his father was wrong—he meant well, and he was trying to steer Casey in the right directions. But right now, Casey wasn't in the mood for hearing one of his father's lectures. He drifted into a daydream, and projected on the truck stop wall was an image of the beautiful snow-capped Rocky Mountains. It was an image he'd only seen in pictures; he'd never been to Colorado, but now he could almost smell the mountain air.

"You look kinda worried," a small voice said.

Casey snapped himself from the daydream and looked to his

left out the open window. A young boy in a baseball uniform stood there staring back, and he almost appeared sympathetic to Casey's situation. "Yeah, I guess I am," Casey said. "My car is broke down..." It seemed rather meaningless to explain anything further to this little boy. He returned his stare to the wall, hoping the mountains would still be there.

"And you're a long way from home, and this is *not* your destination."

Startled by a far more intelligent-sounding remark than he would expect from a youngster like this, Casey quickly shifted his gaze back to the boy. "Yeah, you're right... but how did you know that?"

"I haven't ever seen you around here before."

Casey squinted and relinquished a little smile. "Yeah... you're right again."

"So... why are you so worried?"

Casey took a deep breath and exhaled. "Truth is, my dad said I shouldn't start out on a long trip with this old car, but I did anyway and now he's gonna lecture me about how wrong I was, and *why don't I listen to him?*"

"Oh. So... how far were you planning to go?"

"Another thousand miles... Colorado Springs."

"And you're afraid to call him."

"Not *afraid*. Just tired of hearing *I told you so.*"

"Then don't call him yet. Maybe there's another solution."

Casey stared at the wall and gave that some thought. Perhaps there *were* some other options. Then he looked to the window again, but the boy wasn't there. He leaned out the window to see if the boy was crouched down out of sight. Nothing. Casey got out of the car, walked all around it and scanned the entire parking lot. The boy was nowhere in sight.

Oh well, he thought. It wasn't like the kid was going to solve all his problems, but it would have been good to thank the boy for letting him see his situation in a different light.

Inside the truck stop a thirty-something woman behind the

counter greeted him as he entered, but before he walked the distance from the door, a group of just barely teenagers beat him to the counter with what could have easily been a month's supply of candy, potato chips, and soda. When they had paid for the fare and the cashier had it all bagged, Casey edged up to the counter. The cashier stared at him curiously as if she could sense there was something troubling him. With a sympathetic tone she said, "Can I help you?"

Casey realized then that his expressions must have been easily read, and that he wasn't doing a very good job of concealing the fact that he was alone and vulnerable to his distressful condition. "My old car is broke down, and I'm not from around here. Is there a repair shop anywhere near?"

"Well, there's the new car dealers across the highway, but you might want to try Rudy's in town first."

"How do I find it?"

"It's right on the main street that goes through town. You can't miss it."

"How far?"

"Half a mile."

Casey looked at his watch. It was nearly eight o'clock. "Don't s'pose he's open this late."

"No... probably not. But he's there pretty early in the morning."

"Okay. Thank you." Casey pondered a moment. "Is it okay if I just sleep in my car out back in the parking lot tonight?" He had a tent and a sleeping bag, but driving to the nearest campground could be hazardous to his car's health, and he didn't want to burn up the money he had on a motel room.

"I... I suppose it would be okay," the cashier replied. "Truckers sleep in their trucks out there all the time."

Casey smiled and thanked her again, crossed the room to the entrance of a fast food restaurant and ordered a meatball sub.

2.

The sun shining in his eyes woke Casey from his sleep. He had been dreaming, but he couldn't remember what about. As he slowly shook loose from the cobwebs of sleepiness and regained a cross-section of reality, his first priority was to find a restroom. That accomplished and some cold water splashed on his face to rinse away what remained of his groggy morning condition, his thoughts returned to his ailing car. Progress of his journey to Colorado would be delayed, but for how long he could not be sure. His experience with automobiles told him that the problem was more than just a loose bolt.

He debated on whether to chance driving the car the half-mile into town, or to walk. Here, at least, he knew he had a place to park where no one would bother him if it became necessary to sleep there another night. Weighing the consequences of the car becoming totally disabled halfway to the repair shop, he decided to walk.

Sipping his truck stop coffee from a Styrofoam cup, the walk over the bridge crossing the four lane highway and up a grade on the other side gave him time to reflect on his current state of affairs. All things considered, he decided that he would rather call his friend, Larry, in Colorado for assistance before calling his father. But he wanted to learn of his options to solve the car problem before he did either.

The stretch of Main Street that was also a county highway through town didn't host the buzz of traffic on Saturday morning like it would during the week. Few people were on their way to work, and it was too early for moms to be rushing off to a grocery store or the hair dresser. The sleepy little town was obviously enjoying a quiet weekend at home.

Casey couldn't help but notice the strange array of urban development of this old, rural village. He had walked by a number of last century houses and out buildings that labeled the town as old. But at a certain point at the crest of the hill, where the rest of the town became visible to him, there stood a parade of more modern structures housing business places, but not crowded together like most small town Main Streets are arranged. Prominently accenting the scene was a brilliant, white water tower, its huge globe perched atop a pencil-like pedestal, gleaming in the sunlit, cloudless morning sky. Just beyond the water tower, Casey spotted his destination; the sign next to the road read: *Rudy's Auto Service*. No cars were at the gas pumps, and there didn't seem to be any activity, but a sign in the front window indicated that Rudy was open for business.

Busy with a broom and dustpan, the middle-aged man turned toward the door when Casey entered. "Good morning," he said, his voice genuinely pleasant.

"Good morning," Casey responded, although he didn't think *good* was exactly the best word to describe *his* morning, so far. "Are you Rudy?"

"I am," responded the man.

"The cashier at the truck stop last night said I should see you about my car."

Rudy glanced out the window, scanning the parking lot. Not seeing any unfamiliar vehicles, he looked back to Casey.

"My car isn't here," Casey explained. "It's a 1982 Cutlass. I left it at the truck stop across the highway. It's making some rattling noise and has a bad vibration... didn't think I should drive it any farther in case you couldn't help me."

"How long has it been doing that?" Rudy asked.

"Just a few miles before I got to this exit."

"Well, you'd better try to get it here so I can take a look."

"And if it doesn't make it here?"

"I have a tow truck."

"Okay, great. I'll be back in a little while."

By the time Casey walked back to his car and nursed it the

rest of the way to the garage, Rudy's Auto Service was like the opening hour at a Christmas toy sale. Several customers were lined up waiting their turn at the self-service gas pumps, and several more cars that hadn't been there earlier were parked randomly around the lot, the drivers of which were examining racks of new tires that Rudy had rolled out from the open garage bay doors. He waited patiently until he saw an opportunity to approach Rudy.

"You got really busy all of a sudden," Casey said.

"Saturday mornings can be like that," Rudy replied, seemingly happy with his booming business. "But I'll take a look at your car just as soon as I get these tires mounted." Rudy pointed to the two cars that were already in the garage. "They had appointments for this morning."

"Oh, sure," Casey said. "I understand."

The owners of the two cars getting new tires were a couple of elderly gents, apparently knew each other quite well, and neither were the least bit interested in monitoring the progress on their cars. They stood off to the side chatting about the weather, their gardens, and the honey-do lists their wives had waiting for them. They weren't in any hurry to get home, and they obviously trusted Rudy to do the job right.

Casey had already figured out that he was going to like Rudy. Rudy treated him much differently than his father did; that was to be expected to some degree. But there was something else that set Rudy apart—he didn't look down on Casey as some immature kid. After all, he was about to become a paying customer... if Rudy could fix his problem.

Without any apprehension, Casey strolled into the garage where Rudy was busy dismounting the old tires from the first car. As Rudy tossed the old tire aside, installed a new valve stem, and inspected the empty rim on the tire changing machine, Casey slid one of the new tires off the stack and rolled it to him. Rudy picked it up, set it upright on the rim and swabbed it with the slippery liquid lubricant that would allow the tire to go on the rim with ease. The same procedure repeated three more times, each time Rudy eyeing Casey curiously, if not with a little annoyance.

"I worked in a service station while I went to high school," Casey said. "We had a tire changer just like that. I changed lots of tires."

"Oh?" Rudy said. That seemed to ease his reluctance. "Where was that?"

"Ludington, Michigan."

"What brings you to Wisconsin?"

"I'm on my way to visit my friend in Colorado Springs. Haven't seen him for a year... since we graduated."

"And then your car broke down."

"Yeah."

"Bummer."

Although he thought he should have, Rudy didn't object to Casey's helpful hand while he balanced and installed the next set of tires, nor did Casey consider his assistance an imposition. It was something to do to occupy the time.

"So, you're always this busy?" Casey asked.

"Sometimes," Rudy said. "It used to be a lot busier when the street out front was the main highway. When the bypass was built in '87, the whole town got a little quieter. Of course, this was just a little one-stall garage and gas station then."

"And then you built this new place?"

"After the tornado in '89. Just about the whole town was wiped out."

That explained why Casey had thought the town looked a bit odd—all the old houses on one side of town, and everything new in this part. "Must've been pretty bad," Casey said.

"Yes, it was. We're all pretty lucky, though. It came in the middle of the night—no warning— most of the town was destroyed and only seven people were killed."

"We don't get many tornados where I live."

"Be thankful for that," Rudy said. "If you'd ever been in a

tornado, you'd know what I mean."

"The worst I've ever seen is those God-awful blizzards that blow in from Lake Michigan."

If discussing severe weather conditions can bond a relationship between two people, it certainly did its job that day. When the tires were all balanced and installed on the cars, Rudy had money in his cash drawer, Casey had dirty hands, but it had all happened in harmony.

Unfortunately for Casey, though, it didn't make his car trouble go away. Rudy listened, probed, pried, and inspected the underside of the maroon Cutlass. When he was satisfied that he had checked everything that could be causing the trouble, Casey, too, was ready to accept the bad news.

"Bearings in the transmission," Rudy informed him. "Good thing you stopped when you did... it wouldn't have made it much farther."

"So, what can you do?" Casey asked.

Rudy rubbed his chin. "Rebuilding one of these would probably run about three grand."

"What about a used one from a salvage yard?"

"I can call around and see what's available," Rudy replied. "By the time we get it here and in the car... parts and labor... you'll have about fifteen hundred dollars in it. But I won't know for sure until Monday."

All of Casey's hopes for an easy solution had just darted away. Neither of the options, so far, were appealing, much less acceptable. He didn't have enough money to cover such an expense. But he wasn't ready to give up just yet.

"Is there any place where I can camp for a few days?" he asked Rudy. "I have my tent and a sleeping bag, and there's enough food in my cooler to last the weekend."

"Well, there's Jefferson Park just down this road," Rudy said. "There's bathrooms but no showers or any other facilities. Self-registration... I think ten bucks a night."

"That will do nicely," Casey said.

3.

Rudy's twenty-four-year-old son, Mitchell, who was visiting from Milwaukee, hauled Casey and his camping gear to the park, just a half-mile out of town. Other campers occupied many of the sites, but there were still plenty available. Casey wrote in the required information on one of the self-registration envelopes, inserted the money, and dropped it in the slot of the locked steel box.

"Sure you're gonna be alright?" Mitchell asked him. "Anything you need before I leave?"

Casey thought a long moment, looked around. "Know where I can get some firewood?"

"I can bring some out for you," Mitchell offered.

"Oh, I didn't mean that you should make a special trip just for that."

"It's okay," Mitchell said. "Dad has a year's supply stacked up behind the garage at the house."

"I'll pay you for it," Casey said.

"Forget about it. Dad seems to like you, and I don't think he'll mind. Besides, I helped him cut all that wood, so if I want to give you some..."

"Well that's mighty kind of you, Mitchell. At least I won't have to eat cold beans and hot dogs. Thank you."

"I'll be back in half an hour... anything else you need?"

"No... thanks... I'll be fine with some wood."

When Mitchell returned, Casey was attaching the rain fly to the top of his dome tent. They unloaded a stack of firewood that would be more than ample for the rest of the weekend.

"I have something else for you, too," Mitchell said. From the back seat of his car he retrieved a cold six-pack of *Coca-Cola* and a large bag of potato chips. "I didn't see any of this stuff in your supplies that you brought out before, so I thought you might like some soda and chips."

"Guess I do only have a couple cans of Coke left," Casey admitted. "How much do I owe you for this stuff?"

Mitchell waved his hand as if to dismiss the thought. "Nothing," he said. "That's on me. Maybe I'll stop by sometime this weekend again and have a Coke with you."

"That would be okay," Casey said. "I'd enjoy the company."

Sitting by his crackling campfire that evening, Casey carefully roasted a hot dog skewered onto a long stick, imagining how good a steak would taste, but he didn't have a steak. He was hungry, and even a hot dog, pork and beans, and potato chips would seem like a grand feast.

Quite satisfied after two hot dogs, he sat there mesmerized by the flames dancing above the bed of glowing embers. Images of a broken down car blocked visions of the Colorado Rockies flickering before him. Casey wondered if he would ever see those mountains, or if they would remain just a dream, and Wisconsin, the western-most part of his journey. Now he wished he had not spent so much of his money on shortening the trip by taking the ferryboat across Lake Michigan, but then he realized the breakdown would have occurred somewhere near Chicago had he driven around the lake instead, and this seemed to be a much better alternative than being stranded in Chicago.

"Nice night to sit by the fire," a voice interrupted the scramble of images tumbling around in his head. He hadn't noticed anyone approach, but there sat someone beside him on the ground, knees drawn up to his chest.

At first, Casey was startled by his presence, but quickly determined there was no need for alarm; it was only a harmless little boy. "Yes... it is," he replied, and then he just gazed at the boy, wondering why this urchin had invited himself to share his fire. He studied the blond head of hair and the eyes that twinkled in the firelight. He had seen this boy before. "Hey, you're the boy I saw last night at the truck stop."

The boy didn't answer, just nodded and gave a dimpled little grin.

"You disappeared before I could thank you for helping me to understand my situation—"

"No need to thank me," the boy interrupted. "You would've figured it out on your own."

"Maybe," Casey said. "But I still want to thank you."

The boy stared at the fire. "You're welcome."

"So... are you camping with your family?" Casey asked.

"I was just wandering around and I saw you here... thought you looked like you could use some company."

"Well, thank you... again," Casey returned. "I appreciate it. I don't know exactly what I need right now. My car is beyond repairs that I can't afford, and I'm still a thousand miles from where I'm supposed to be."

"Maybe *this* is where you're supposed to be... not Colorado. Maybe your car breaking down here is an omen."

"An *omen*?" Casey thought about that, and then he eyed the boy with curiosity. "How did you know I was going to Colorado?"

"You said so last night at the truck stop."

"Oh."

"Sometimes you need to pay more attention to what fate drops in your lap... like your car breaking down here."

"My car breaking down ruined my plans for the whole summer."

"It didn't necessarily *ruin* your plans... it just *changed* them."

The boy's ability to turn negatives into positives continued to amaze Casey. Once again, because of the little boy's wisdom, Casey began to grasp an entirely different perspective on his predicament. Perhaps this *was* the way to show his father that he could do something on his own that turned out right. He wasn't quite sure how that would materialize, but he had time to give it some thought.

Just then he heard car tires crunching the gravel on the roadway through the campground. He turned to look.

Headlights approached, stopped by his campsite and went out. He recognized Mitchell's car.

"Thought I'd come and have that Coke with you," Mitchell said as he stepped over to the fire.

"Hi, Mitchell," Casey greeted his guest. "I'm glad you came. I'll get one out of the cooler for you." Then he turned to where the boy sat. "Would you like a Coke, too?"

But the boy was gone.

"Who are you talking to?" Mitchell asked, not seeing anyone else by the fire.

"I was just talking to a young boy who came over to keep me company for a while, but now he's gone."

"I must've scared him off," Mitchell said. "What's his name? Maybe I know him."

Casey thought a moment, and then realized he had never asked the boy's name. "I don't know... he never said." He walked over to his tent, unzipped the door and reached in for two cans of soda from his cooler. When he handed Mitchell the cold can, he gazed around the darkened campground. "I think he's camping with his family. He probably went back," he said, and then sat down beside Mitchell by the fire.

"Dad says you were on your way to Colorado."

"Yeah, and then my stupid old car broke down."

"Well, your car is in good hands," Mitchell said. "My dad is the best mechanic—"

"That's great," Casey interrupted. "The only problem is that I don't have enough money to fix the car."

"So, what are you gonna do?"

"Don't know for sure... yet. D'ya suppose there are any jobs for me around here anywhere?"

Mitchell chuckled a little. "There isn't much of anything around Ripley anymore... not since the tornado nearly wiped out the whole town. That was fifteen years ago, and that's why I'm going to Aviation Mechanics school in Milwaukee."

"Your dad mentioned something to me about a tornado... said

that's why most of the town is new."

"Yeah," Mitchell said. "I was only nine, and I wasn't even home when it happened... was on a canoe trip up in the Boundary Waters with the Boy Scouts. But I sure remember what this town looked like when we came home."

"Pretty bad, huh?"

"Bad isn't the word for it. By the time we came back a couple of days after the storm, they had cleared the rubble from some of the streets with bulldozers so they could get through with the emergency vehicles. But you wouldn't believe the mess... and the stink."

"Stink?"

"A mixture of sewer, rotten garbage, manure, diesel fuel, swamp mud, dead animals... every bad smell you can possibly imagine hung in the air for days."

"Must've been awful," Casey said. "Was your house destroyed?"

"Only part of it... the part where my bedroom was. If I hadn't been on that Boy Scout outing... if I would've been home... I would've been killed."

"But everyone must've taken cover... didn't they?"

"It came just after midnight. Everyone in a small town is in bed sleeping at midnight. And the power was out because of lightning earlier that night, so the weather siren didn't work. There was virtually no warning. The only reason there weren't more people killed was just plain luck... or a miracle."

"Yeah, your dad said that only, what? Seven people were killed."

Mitchell bowed his head. It was obvious that a sorrowful memory had resurfaced. He looked up at Casey and nodded. "One of them was my best friend."

"I'm sorry," Casey said, apologizing for causing him to remember.

"Cody Miller's mom couldn't afford to send him on the canoe trip, and she refused the *charity* when we all offered to chip in so

18

he could go with us."

Casey didn't know what to say. He sensed that years ago Mitchell had worked his way past the   tears when remembering his friend, but remembering still caused a heavy heart.

"She died a few years ago at a mental hospital... had been there since right after Cody's funeral. I used to go see her occasionally, but her condition reached a point that she didn't even know me anymore."

Casey looked into Mitchell's face with admiration. "I don't know what I'd do if I lost my best friend like that."

The two of them sat staring into the fire for several minutes without speaking. Mitchell finally broke the silence: "So, you think you wanna stay around here and find a job?"

"It's my best option right now," Casey replied.

"Can't you call your parents? Wouldn't they help you out?"

"I could, but I don't want to," Casey said. "I need to prove to my dad that I can do *something* right... on my own."

"Oh, I get it," Mitchell said. "You don't get along with him very well?"

"We get along just fine. He just thinks I'm helpless and irresponsible, and I have to show him that I'm neither of those things."

"What kind of job do you want?"

"Don't know... haven't thought about it yet."

"What did you do before you came here?"

"Worked at *McDonald's* for a year after high school. Pumped gas and fixed flat tires at a gas station before that."

"Well... we don't have a *McDonald's* here."

"Actually, that's good. I hated it. It's why I decided to go to Colorado."

"My dad knows a lot of people. Maybe he can scare something up for you."

4.

Casey walked through the entire campground Sunday afternoon watching inconspicuously as several families packed their gear and loaded their cars to head for home after a weekend of fresh air, over-cooked hamburgers, and mosquito repellant. Not a single youngster among them matched the young boy that had visited him the night before. Apparently, he and his family had left earlier than Casey had begun observing.

It was a day he could sit back and relax; there was nothing he could do about his car; there was nothing he could do about *anything*. Until he could get back to his car where the charger for his cell phone lay in the glove compartment, he couldn't call his buddy in Colorado Springs; the phone battery was nearly dead. Didn't seem much point in calling Larry now, anyway, until he knew for certain what his plans would be. If this did become a temporary home, he'd have to come up with a good explanation why Larry was taking a back seat to this half-baked idea that Casey could prove something to his father in this middle-of-nowhere little town in Southwestern Wisconsin. Larry was his best friend, and nothing had ever come between them before... until Larry's dad moved the family to Colorado.

By Sunday evening, the entire campground was nearly deserted except for Casey and a few other stragglers that didn't seem to care that the weekend was over. Casey didn't see anyone there who he wanted to socialize with; he made a fire and ate his hot dogs, beans and potato chips alone.

There didn't seem to be any reason for a big rush on Monday morning to get into town. Rudy would need some time to make a few phone calls, and he would certainly have other customers to tend to as well. To his pleasant surprise, when he arrived at nine o'clock, Mitchell was there, too, outside the garage scrubbing the tow truck with a long-handled brush he dipped frequently into a bucket of hot, soapy water.

"Hi, Mitchell," he greeted.

"Good morning, Casey." Mitchell put down the brush, grabbed a water hose and sprayed the soap suds off the truck. "How did the camping work out?"

"It's great," Casey replied. "Lots of mosquitoes at night, but as long as I kept a smoky fire going, it wasn't too bad."

Casey's Oldsmobile was parked out in the lot now; Rudy had said he would leave it in the garage over the weekend to ensure the security of Casey's personal belongings left in the car, but now the garage was busy again and moving it outside had become necessary. Casey stared at it a long moment. "I need to get my phone charger," he said to Mitchell. "Is my car locked?"

"Keys are in the office," Mitchell replied. "I'll get them for you."

"Mitch!" Rudy called out, and then he met his son just outside the garage door. "Would you take the truck and tow Mrs. Carlson's car here from her house?"

"Sure. What's wrong with it?"

"Won't start."

"Why don't we just jump-start it?"

"She insists that we tow it in and fix it. It probably just needs another new battery."

"Hey, Dad. Would it be okay if Casey rides along?"

Rudy glanced at Casey standing alone and forlorn next to the tow truck. "Sure... why not?"

Mitchell retrieved the Oldsmobile keys and handed them off to Casey. "While your phone is charging, if you want, you can ride with me in the truck to pick up Ida Carlson's car."

Grateful for Mitchell's offer, Casey grinned. "Okay. I'll plug in my phone." He unlocked the car door, found the charger in the glove compartment and plugged it into the cigarette lighter.

On the way across town to Mrs. Carlson's house, Casey took

notice of all the modern homes, and then several blocks farther, it appeared as if they had transitioned into another era. Old homes—some simple salt box and cat slide roofs, among more elegant Victorians and Italianates.

"Tornado must not have touched this part of town," Casey said.

Remembering that he had given a brief mention of Ripley's 1989 tornado experience, Mitchell continued with more detail. "It was a category five... the strongest ever recorded anywhere around here... went right through the middle of town. Leveled everything in its path, including the entire downtown businesses, fire station, old railroad depot, homes... everything. Only thing left standing intact was the new water tower. Our house was right on the edge... only got damaged partially, but our neighbors across the street lost everything."

"Wow," Casey replied. "It's really amazing that so few people died."

"Ida Carlson—the car we're picking up—she lived in the most gorgeous hundred-year-old house in the part of town that was hit the hardest. Her brother, Jim Engle, was visiting for a few days, helping her with some maintenance on her beautiful old house. He was killed."

"How did it happen that she survived?"

"They dug her out of the rubble early the next morning... covered up by her bed mattress... hardly a scratch."

"Amazing."

"Mrs. Carlson is one of the few who didn't build a new house... just moved into another old one on the other side of town. Said she was too old to build a new house... wouldn't be around long enough to enjoy it." Mitchell laughed. "That was fifteen years ago."

Casey felt a strange sort of closeness to this town; he had never been near it before, and he knew no one—except for his brief acquaintance with Rudy and Mitchell. But he suddenly felt some odd connection, for which there was no reasonable explanation.

Mrs. Carlson's old two-story Victorian house was every bit as pristine as Mitchell had described the one demolished years ago by the killer twister. The unattached garage at the end of a long driveway shrouded by huge oak trees stood just beyond the house with its swing doors open exposing a moss green Ford Torino. As old as it was, it shined like a brand new car.

"I don't know why she even keeps this car," Mitchell said. "It hardly ever gets driven, and every winter, the battery freezes up, and Dad has to put in a new one every summer."

While Mitchell got the Torino situated on the tow truck lift, a stooped, wrinkled, white-haired woman came to watch. "Now Mitchell," she said. "You tell your father to take good care of this car."

"Yes, Ida, I will," Mitchell replied.

"It was Jim's car, you know," the old woman added.

"Dad will make it like new again, Ida," Mitchell reassured her. "And then we'll bring it back and put it in the garage again, okay?"

"Oh, thank you, Mitchell," Ida Carlson said. She patted his shoulder. "You're such a sweet boy."

As they rode away with the Torino in tow, Mitchell said, "She tells me that every time."

"What? That you're *such a sweet boy?*"

Mitchell's face turned a little red. "Well, that, too, but every time she tells me that it was Jim's car."

"Jim was her brother who was killed?"

"Yeah."

"But wouldn't his car have been wrecked by the tornado?"

"The pickup truck that he drove here was smashed beyond recognition. They found it two blocks away from Ida's house a couple of days after the storm. His wife in Milwaukee didn't want to keep this car, and Ida—of course—needed one because hers was wrecked, too. So she got Jim's Torino, and it's been babied and pampered ever since."

The giant oaks, white picket fences and pillared verandahs of the old part of town gave way to the sprawling ranch and split-levels, manicured lawns and trimmed hedges of the new. A tingle slid down Casey's spine when he imagined all those grand old houses that once lined these streets strewn in twisted heaps of rubble and trash, and their occupants roaming hopelessly about trying to make sense of it all. But fifteen years had obviously healed the wounds, and Ripley appeared to be back, alive and well.

5.

"**M**itch tells me you might want to stay in Ripley and get a job here."

"Yes, sir," Casey replied. "I've given that some thought over the weekend."

"Ain't much around here for a young fella like you, y' know," Rudy warned.

It was true; there was very little in a small rural town to keep a youngster like Casey entertained. But Casey was determined to make the best of his deplorable situation, and he was determined to prove that he could make a responsible decision. It was as if he were punishing himself for not listening to good advice when it was offered by his father.

"I know that, but I think it might be my best option right now," Casey said. "I don't have a car, but everything in a small town is close enough that I might not *need* one for a while. I can stay at the campground until I find a job and a place to live."

"I found a used transmission for your car," Rudy said.

"Oh?"

"A salvage yard near Rockford has a good one. I can get it trucked over here day after tomorrow. Couple of days after that and about nine hundred bucks… you can be on your way to Colorado."

"Nine hundred?"

"Give or take."

Now Casey had another option, albeit not one that would bail him out of his predicament completely. "Well," he said with some reluctance. "That's kind of a tough decision. If I do that, I won't have enough left *to get to Colorado*… or anyplace else, for that matter."

Mitchell intervened. "Dad… do you think he could get a job here?"

Rudy pondered on the thought a long moment. "Well… if he

really wants to stay in Ripley, I guess there's a possibility."

"Do you know someone who might hire me?" Casey asked. "After I work for a while, then I'd fix the car—"

"Or get a different one," Mitchell interrupted. "You might want to think about putting that much money into that old car."

"Good point," Casey said. "I'll think on that."

"Come over tomorrow morning," Rudy said. "I'll let you know what I find out about a job."

"Okay. I'll be here," Casey replied with enthusiasm. "Right now, I'm going over to the grocery store and pick up some food and a bag of ice. I'll see you tomorrow."

"Wait," Mitchell said. "I'll give you a ride. The ice will melt before you get back to the campground."

6.

Casey was up at first light the next morning. He bathed the best he could with a wash cloth and a bar of soap at the campground bathroom sink. If he were to meet with a prospective employer, he wanted to look his best. He could possibly make a commitment this day that would change the course of his life.

By seven o'clock Casey had walked into town and was at Rudy's Auto Service. "Good morning, Rudy," he said as he opened the door. "Am I too early?"

"No, not at all," Rudy replied looking up from his desk behind the counter. "In fact, I'm glad you're here before it gets too busy... so we can talk."

To Casey, that could mean only one thing: Rudy had some good news about available jobs in the area. He didn't want to think about the probability of total rejection.

"Mitch told me you worked at a *McDonald's* before you came here, but you told me you worked in a gas station fixing tires."

"Oh, I did both. *McDonald's* came *after* high school."

"I see. So would you rather work at a fast food restaurant, or get your hands dirty?"

"I'd rather get my hands dirty," Casey said with a smile.

"Do you remember everything about tire repair? And how to use the tire changing machine?"

Casey started to catch on to where this conversation was headed; this was an interview! "Yes, sir," he said with confidence. "It's kinda like riding a bicycle... I didn't forget."

"Would you be satisfied with a part-time position to begin with?"

"Sure... if it's enough to get me a bed to sleep in and two or three meals a day... sure I'd be satisfied."

"How does ten dollars an hour, about twenty hours a week sound to you? To start with?"

"Are you offering me a job here, Sir?"

"Yes, I am. Since Mitch went off to school in Milwaukee, I realized that I missed having him around, and I've been thinking I could use some extra help now and then."

"I'll do the best job I know how, Sir. I won't let you down."

"First of all," Rudy said. "Let's get one thing straight."

"What's that, sir?"

"That you'll quit calling me *sir*. You'll call me *Rudy* like everyone else."

"Yes, sir... I mean yes, Rudy."

"That's better. Now... when can you start?"

"When do you want me to start?"

"Yesterday."

"What should I do first?"

"Fill out this paperwork for your tax deductions. My bookkeeper will need to know a few particulars. Then I'll have Mitch show you where everything is... tools and stuff... and then you can put a new battery in Mrs. Carlson's Torino."

7.

Working for Rudy came with rewards Casey had not expected. Rudy put him in contact with an elderly retired couple—Don and Julia Hoff—who rented him a furnished apartment in the upstairs of their house. It was quite small, but adequate, and only a hundred dollars a month—just a little supplement to their Social Security. They didn't require any deposits—only a promise to be quiet at night.

Mitchell helped him move in a couple of days before he went back to Milwaukee. Mitchell had taken a week off from his summer job to spend some time in his hometown with family. It had gone by much too quickly.

Casey realized that he had been quite fortunate to share so much of Mitchell's time. Most of Mitchell's schoolmates had left the small town, too, in search of bigger and better things, just as Mitchell had done. He had found his place in a good school and a good job in the big city, and now he had to return to his big city life. Casey would miss him. Mitchell had been a good friend.

Working for Rudy, though, exposed Casey to just about everyone in the small town. Even though his gas pumps weren't the only ones there, most of the local people preferred doing business with Rudy, rather than the less personal touch they received from the large corporation convenience store located out at the four-lane exit. That one couldn't fix a flat tire or change their oil or tune up a poorly-running car. But Rudy could do all those things, and more, and the local people appreciated the friendly service he offered most of all.

During lunches and breaks, and sometimes when there just wasn't anything else going on, Casey was entertained by Rudy's answers to his questions about Ripley—especially the stories about Ripley's tornado history. Casey was fascinated with the chain of events that occurred that fateful night in 1989. Maybe it was the excitement of adventure; maybe it was the drama; maybe it was miraculous outcome; or maybe it was simply that human element—the bravery and conscientious reactions of those who faced the disaster with courage and faith. Whatever it was, it fascinated Casey.

Rudy told of how he was not feeling well that afternoon, the real reason he had missed the Little League baseball game—the first one he'd missed all season. "I went home that evening, only looking forward to resting in my recliner. I tried to sleep, but then a thunderstorm erupted and the thunder and lightning kept me from a sound rest. Then the power went off; we sat in the dark with only candles for light, until my wife walked me up to bed.

"Mitch was away on a Boy Scout outing at the Boundary Waters, and a lucky thing, too. Just past midnight, I was awakened by a terrific roar—like a freight train coming through my living room. There had been no warning siren... I guess because of the power outage, so the abrupt noise was rather mysterious and startling. In the short time that I gathered my senses and could hustle me and my wife to the basement, the twister was there... ripping the town to shreds. Of course, we didn't know... we weren't aware right then just how bad it was.

"And then, just a half a minute later, all was quiet again... deathly quiet. But that didn't last long; soon after, I could hear voices shouting and crying and even screaming. I told Maria to stay put in the safety of the basement while I went up to investigate. It was so dark that I could see nothing, but I sensed that something was terribly wrong, because I could feel the outside air. Half of our house—the side with Mitchell's bedroom was gone; the kitchen and utility room were gone.

"I felt my way through the rubble, listening to the shouts and screams from my neighbors. My only concern right then was to get to my garage and my service truck where I would find my big emergency flashlight. But it was difficult going; I couldn't see any familiar things to guide me, and there was so much rubble on the ground it was hard to even walk.

"When I finally made it here to the garage, the garage was non-existent. Everything was gone. Nothing was here but a bare concrete slab that had been the garage floor."

Casey was mesmerized. "But you still couldn't see the total destruction of the tornado."

"No," Rudy continued. "But I had a pretty good idea by what I had experienced so far." He pointed across the street. "There used to be a grocery store right over there. I headed in that direction, thinking I would break into it. I knew they had a good stock of flashlights and batteries, and I knew where to find them. But I didn't have to break in; the front wall of the store was completely gone. I fumbled around in the rubble inside the store until I found them. It was quite a relief to have a little light again. But of course, it wasn't a pleasant sight that the light showed me.

"My bulk fuel tank truck lay upside down in the street about a block that way, and my service truck and wrecker were mangled under what appeared to be the roof of someone's house down in that direction. I knew the best I could do right then was to see if I could give assistance to anyone who needed help. There was nothing of my place left to save."

Rudy went on to tell of the mass confusion that seemed to control the remainder of the night. Somehow, word had gotten out to neighboring towns, and ambulances arrived, but there was no way into town; the road from the four-lane by-pass was completely blocked. Fire and rescue trucks sat helplessly at the edge of town, their crews only able to walk in with whatever tools and equipment they could carry. Many injured victims were dug out of the rubble and carried to the waiting ambulances, and unfortunately, some of those victims did not make it to the ambulances alive.

Casey recalled Mitchell's sorrowful memory of his best friend. "What happened to Cody Miller?" Casey asked. "Mitchell told me about his best friend who was killed that night."

"One of the rescuers found Cody and his mother in the wreckage of their house. His mother was able to walk to the ambulance, and the rescuer carried Cody... but Cody Miller died in his arms before he got there... a severe head injury."

Customers would come in occasionally and overhear Rudy's accounts of the storm, and they would sometimes fill in a few more details. Even though it had been fifteen years earlier, it seemed that the worst nightmare the town had ever known could not be forgotten. Although it was a bad memory, it was a heartwarming story of how the people of the town came together, to help each other, to combat the adversity, to mend the wounds, to heal the pain, to mourn the lost loved ones, to recover and to rebuild. They never gave up hope, and all but a very few stayed to see the rebirth of their town they all loved.

.

8.

"**Y**our mother and I will drive over there and pick you up tomorrow."

It wasn't exactly what Casey had expected to hear when he finally found the courage to call his father. "No, Dad. I'm staying here... for a while, at least... until I can afford to do something about my car."

"I can send you money to fix your car—"

"No, Dad. I have a good job and a place to live. I'll earn the money myself, and maybe I'll buy a different car... but please... I don't want your help this time. I'm gonna do it on my own terms."

"What about Colorado? Larry?"

"Larry and Colorado will just have to wait."

When Casey finally convinced his dad that he wasn't leaving Ripley just yet, he said his good-byes, and pressed the button on his cell phone to disconnect the call. He felt good about what he had just accomplished. He knew his father was probably suffering from shock just about now over what his son had just told him, but he would recover.

9.

Saturday. Casey had only worked half the day; Rudy generally always closed the shop at noon on Saturdays unless there was something urgent that came up, and on this Saturday, nothing had.

The last full week in July had been blistering hot and dry, and now, after seven straight days with temperatures in the upper nineties, the forecast promised rain. Heavy, warm, moist air moving in from the southwest was about to collide with cooler air from the north, and the collision was due to occur over Northeast Iowa and Southwest Wisconsin later that day. The problem with air masses of this nature coming together abruptly is that it usually produces severe thunderstorms, and this one had all the characteristics of a blockbuster. Although the rain would be a welcomed relief, no one was particularly eager to see damaging winds and hail as the weathermen were anticipating.

Casey was still debating on whether he should spend nine hundred dollars on his old car, or buy a different one. He had nearly saved up enough to fix the Oldsmobile without hurting his financial status. It was the first and only car he had ever owned, and he liked it. But maybe it was time to let go... to splurge on something else. He had seen plenty of older cars for sale that he could afford, and Rudy would certainly help him choose a good, dependable model.

But it was still a hard decision to make.

Rather than going to his upstairs apartment that was bound to be hot and uncomfortable, Casey changed into a pair of shorts and T-shirt at the shop and walked to the Log Cabin Family Restaurant about three blocks up the street to have lunch. The TV mounted on the wall above the counter where he usually sat was tuned in to the Weather Channel, as everyone was interested in the developing storms that threatened the entire area. Casey could sense uncertain tension, wondering if these were similar conditions as in 1989, and people were remembering.

At present, though, the sky was only partly cloudy, but the heat and lack of any breeze at all had most of the town's residents soaking up the air conditioning wherever it was available. The Log Cabin was nearly filled to capacity during this lunch hour.

Casey knew he shouldn't spend too long in the restaurant; going out in the heat again would just be that much worse the longer he stayed in the air conditioned room. He ate his cheeseburger and French fries, ordered a large, icy *Coke* to go, and headed to a park bench under some trees where he liked to just sit and think. On the opposite side of the road, down about a block and a half was the Public Library. It was open all day, and if the weather got too bad, he could always find shelter there. Instead of the bench, though, today he decided to stretch out on the cooler grass under the tree.

He lay there thinking about how his life had turned around since he had arrived in Ripley. Before, he'd had very little sense of direction, never knowing where he was going beyond the next day, mainly because his father had been far too protective—not that he didn't appreciate his dad's caring about him. But it had hindered him from learning his real capabilities. In the past two months he had discovered so much about himself, and now he had the confidence to move forward; to make sound decisions... and then he drifted off into a comfortable nap.

10.

Casey came awake abruptly to the deafening drone of a siren. He sat up. He didn't know how long he had been sleeping, but it must've been quite a while because all the ice in his soda was melted. He drank it anyway—he was thirsty.

He gazed at the horizons all around him. Dark, menacing clouds loomed everywhere. After about a minute, the siren stopped. There still didn't seem to be an immediate threat of rain, although the clouds to the southwest were boiling with something, and heavy weather wasn't far away. He looked toward the library building. He could sprint that distance in under a minute if he had to. The air was cooler now, and it felt good to just sit there and enjoy the slight breeze that had kicked up. Cars still hummed along the road at the thirty-five mile per hour speed limit, but there were fewer now than earlier. Traffic on the four-lane seemed lighter than usual, too. He thought about heading to the library.

A couple of minutes later, the siren atop the fire station sounded again with its long and persistent rollercoaster drone. The wind had picked up some, and the sky had darkened drastically; it was becoming more obvious by the second that the bad weather had arrived. Casey jumped to his feet and turned toward the library. He could hear, now, a tremendous roar like he had never heard before. As he started for the shelter, he stopped dead in his tracks and stared. He'd never seen a tornado before, either, but what he was staring at didn't need a sign to identify it. The funnel had touched down at the four-lane exit ramp, and in that brief next moment Casey knew that it was coming his way. It was still way beyond the safety of the library shelter, but he hesitated, wondering if he could make it there safely before the tornado did. And then he saw another sight that was nearly unbelievable: in the middle of the road between him and the library stood a small boy all alone, apparently frozen with fear at the sight of the black, spinning, roaring monster. He studied the boy just briefly. It was *that* boy. The same boy who had appeared at his window the night his car broke down; the same blond-haired boy who visited him at his campfire.

He couldn't just leave the boy standing there—he would be killed! Casey had to do something.

"HEY!" he yelled to the boy, but there was no response. The boy just stood there staring at the fast-approaching twister. Without any more hesitation, Casey darted toward him. Perhaps he could grab the boy and get to the library shelter in time. It was his only hope.

He had almost reached the boy when he caught sight of something flying toward him. A quick glance to his left identified a tree branch, and by the time Casey could maneuver to avoid it, the broken limb knocked him off his feet. He went down on the pavement on one knee and he tried to break his fall with his right hand that scrubbed along the concrete. His hand burning with pain, he looked up to see the boy standing over him, and now the twister was between them and the library. There would be no chance to reach the shelter.

The boy helped Casey to his feet and pointed off to the right. The roar of the tornado was so loud there was no use trying to talk. Casey quickly looked where the boy was pointing. There, on the embankment slanting upward away from the roadway was the opening of a concrete culvert about three feet in diameter, large enough to crawl into. Casey could barely put his weight on his right leg, but a brief glance over his shoulder told him there was only a matter of seconds available to reach that culvert. He limped to it and with help from the boy tugging on his good hand from inside, he slipped in just as a swirling mass of dust and debris engulfed the end of the culvert.

They sat there, well back from the opening, staring in awe at the circle of dim light, and in a few more seconds everything went silent.

They waited. When the calmness seemed to be lasting, Casey inched his way to the opening and peeked out. The boy crawled up beside him.

"Uh-oh," the boy said and pointed up the street toward Rudy's.

There, in the middle of the street, among all sorts of trash, lay a maroon car upside down, the roof smashed down to the level of the hood and trunk. It was Casey's Oldsmobile.

"Looks like you don't have to wonder about buying a new car now," the blond-haired boy said.

Casey just stared, attempting to grasp the reality of the circumstances. Gazing around the immediate vicinity, there didn't seem to be a great amount of damage other than a couple of uprooted trees, numerous tree limbs littering the open spaces along with garbage cans, roof shingles, and other unidentifiable debris... and Casey's overturned car. All the buildings seemed to still be intact.

"Everything's going to be okay for you now, Casey," the boy said softly. "So I have to go now." He crawled out of the tube.

"Wait!" Casey said. "You just saved my life and I don't even know your name."

The boy turned back toward Casey. "Cody. Cody Miller," he said with a sad sort of smile. And then he was gone.

Casey didn't watch to see where the boy went. There was no need.

HOUSE
OF
MANY
ROOMS

J.L. FREDRICK

HOUSE OF MANY ROOMS
J.L. Fredrick

I HAD RECENTLY MOVED to a small town near the Wisconsin River. There were several reasons for that particular move, the most prevalent of which was to escape from the city's nerve endings that seemed to always be twitching. I had grown from infant to teen in the country, and I longed to return.

I chose a quaint little one bedroom cottage home at the edge of the small town. It was perfect for me; it offered the country quiet and solitude for which I had been longing—that peaceful, non-distracting environment that is so beneficial to a writer. A novel that still remained unfinished after nearly two years occupied space in my computer; new surroundings, I was certain, would rekindle my creative flames.

Another reason to choose that particular locale was to satisfy my curiosity about the many historically significant nooks along the river; most were now obscured by time; many were just barely recognizable; some, I had read, were haunted. During the territorial development, the river continued to be one of the main arteries for transportation. Along its banks sprouted trading posts and inns that provided supplies and shelter to weary travelers. It was those inns—or taverns, as they were called in the pioneer times—that helped fuel the legends; that in later years harbored the ghosts and ogres and demons within their decaying attics and cellars until there was nothing left but the rubble of ruins that would eventually be completely

43

consumed by nature. But if there *was* something left, I wanted to find it.

I had possession of an old journal that was given to me by a former neighbor, who had obtained it with a box of miscellaneous junk at a yard sale many years prior. She knew I was deeply interested in historical matters, and because the old book was of no value to her, Deborah offered it to me. I briefly inspected the volume; an inch-thick mass of browned, brittle paper was sandwiched between worn leather-clad covers, a color of something between dead oak leaves and oatmeal. Their fortitude, however, had preserved the integrity of the pages, and although faded, the penned handwriting was legible in pleasantly elegant penmanship. As I carefully turned the pages back to the front inside cover, I discovered the author's name, Horatio P. Tripp, and apparently the date he began the journal, August 1, 1901.

Offering to pay Deborah for her find—which she refused in neighborly fashion—I graciously accepted the antique document, unaware, then, that I was holding the key to a mystery so incredible, so bizarre, so unbelievable, that no man living in current times could imagine its depth with even a fragment of reality.

Months passed while the old journal occupied space on a book shelf, occasionally finding its way to my desk. At first, I merely scanned the pages for some key elements that would indicate where Horatio P. Tripp resided when he scribed the entries. If this were the writings of Tripp's existence in Pennsylvania or New York or some other faraway place, and had been carried here by virtue of a move, the book would have been of less interest to me. But the text occasionally referred to "the river," and "the mill;" it drew me in until I was scrutinizing every word, and then a name appeared that supplied the missing link— *Dekorra*. I immediately recognized the pioneer town on the bank of the Wisconsin River whose dot on the map is now only a memory. Horatio P. Tripp had been a young boy when Dekorra was a thriving community, and as a person intrigued by local pioneer history, I was vaguely familiar with its short-lived existence.

Quite consistently appearing as anniversaries of events in his life, Tripp dated his entries beginning in August, 1901. He had been too young—only 12—at the beginning of the Civil War, so when the local Guard marched off to war, young Horatio was left behind with the important task of guarding the home front.

He told of the constant downstream flow of lumber rafts on the river, thousands upon thousands of board feet of pine lumber cut from the northern forests, silently guided down the river by the skilled, red-shirted raftsmen. He told of the steady horse- and oxen-drawn wagon traffic into Dekorra hauling corn and wheat to the flourmill. He told of the hotels and stores; he told of the blacksmith shop and the boot shop; he told of the barrooms and the bloody fights that sometimes erupted in them when a rowdy bunch of lumber rafters stopped for a night. He wrote about the residents, and their houses that varied from meager shacks to elegant mansions surrounded by flowerbeds, apple trees and weeping willows.

And then his narrative shifted to a sadder time when the railroad bypassed the village by many miles; businesses closed, one by one, relocating in other communities where the railroad offered more convenient overland transport of goods. Families uprooted and moved with them, and eventually, Dekorra dwindled to almost nothing.

Horatio P. Tripp, however, remained, working adjacent farmland that he inherited from his father. He had lived his entire life there, and he refused to leave. And so his journal jumped forward to October 13, 1901 when his stories took on the tone of his present time.

After setting the journal aside to resume work on *my* current novel project, some weeks later I picked up where I had left Horatio roaming the rolling hills along the Wisconsin River, hunting I presumed, as he mentioned toting a gun, and he was accompanied by his trusty yellow dog, Spike. I gathered that Spike was a noted hunter, with a well-known reputation for proficiency. It was the fall of the year; the crops were harvested, and on the 26th of October there was nothing better to do than hunt. Horatio seemed to be quite familiar with the area, but on that particular day, he noticed something he had never seen before. Tucked into a wide, rocky ravine leading away from the river was a house. No road led to the house that he could see, so it wasn't surprising that he had not seen it until now, but it still seemed odd to him that he was unaware, because he had hunted this area many times in the past. Perhaps, he thought, leaves on the surrounding trees had hidden it before, but the trees had undressed early that year, their foliage lying brown and lifeless at their feet like a pile of dirty laundry.

Horatio had walked to the house that appeared abandoned, investigating its presence that piqued his curiosity. Obviously, no one had lived there in a long time, as there were no signs of life or any evidence that human activity had been recently present. He described the structure as plain and simple square design, two story, non-ornate, charcoal gray from the lack of paint, and it reeked of rotting wood.

The remainder of that entry, October 26, 1901, was rather strange. Horatio suddenly sounded deranged, as if something horrific had frightened him. *"It is the work of the devil,"* he said. *"Anyone coming near that house of many rooms should beware."*

His entry of the next day, October 27, was less intense, but apparently, Spike had disappeared during the previous day's adventure, and when Horatio returned to the site of the *house of many rooms* to look for him, the house had vanished, with no trace of it ever being there. Horatio was absolutely certain he had been searching the right spot. He was heartbroken over the loss of his dog, but he dared not tell anyone of his experience for fear of being imprisoned at an asylum for the insane.

Throughout the entire writings, Horatio P. Tripp occasionally mentioned casually of his wanderings back to that place, and it remained void of any structures... until... October 26, 1902. On that day, the old decrepit edifice stood as it had exactly one year ago, to the day. Horatio wouldn't go near it, just gazed from a distance, and vowed never to set foot on that ground again.

I quickly skipped forward through the old book to satisfy my curiosity. The page where I found the October 26, 1903 entry by Horatio P. Tripp rendered exactly what I expected. He had gone to the place and once more viewed from afar that old house that had been absent for the past 364 days.

My first reaction was to re-read every passage of the journal that pertained to any sight or contact with this mysterious old house. I wanted to be certain that nothing had been overlooked or missed. The second reading produced little more than the first, and I was sure that everything Horatio P. Tripp said was well-understood. He had clearly been frightened during his first visit to the old house, so intensely that he vowed never to set foot on that soil again. But his narration did not indicate *what* had threatened his soul to such a degree.

By simple deduction, I decided that Horatio must have entered the house (although he didn't specifically say that he had) because he spoke of "many rooms." He could not have known that unless he was inside. But what had he entered? A mirage? His own hallucination? A product of his imagination?

It was in my best interest to at least look for the place; Horatio's description of the landscape indicated rough, rocky terrain that would not be suitable for cropland, or desirable as a modern day building site. Perhaps the location would still be preserved as Horatio P. Tripp had seen it in 1903. The following Saturday, a nice sunny September day, I set out to find the site of Horatio P. Tripp's *house of many rooms.*

After roaming the general area that Tripp described, I located several natural landmarks he had mentioned, so I felt confident that I was in the right vicinity. But several hours later, I had not found the craggy ravine. My discouragement had nearly taken its toll on the effort, and I was ready to call it quits for the day when I found myself standing in the midst of the very setting to which Horatio had sworn never to return. I knew it was the right spot; a strange aura seemed to engulf the little valley, and it was easy to understand, now, why it had been undetected. Time and nature had disguised it with a growth of trees and underbrush, tall weeds and vines. Where I stood, though, was a clearing thirty feet across—no trees, no brush, and a scarce few orphan blades of grass.

The eerie quality of strangeness brought the hair on my arms to bristle; the tingle at the back of my neck descended my spine, and then crawled down my legs to the tips of my toes. Absolutely nothing was there to be physically afraid of, yet, I sensed an urgent desire to move out of the clearing.

Back at home, I called Mark, a buddy since junior high school. He lived in Tennessee now, but his roots were still in Wisconsin, although lately, he had spent very little time here. As youngsters we had shared so many wild adventures, explored so many unknown places, and laughed in the face of so many dangers together. Mark was always game for a thrill, and extraordinarily intrigued with the supernatural. It seemed only fitting to invite Mark to join me on an incredible escapade, for which the early stages of a plan were tumbling around in my head.

When I told Mark about the journal and my quest, he was ready and willing to pack a suitcase and catch the next flight. "No, not now," I said. "We have to wait until October 26th."

Very little planning was necessary. As long as Mark knew he should be prepared for hiking, everything else would fall into line. We would leave my place at dawn. As kids, Mark and I had embarked on many exploration adventures at that time of day, so this would be just like old times. If my suspicions were correct, the house would reappear again on October 26th... or it wouldn't. Either way, Mark and I could spend some quality time together, something we hadn't done lately.

Mark's plane from Memphis arrived on time the afternoon of October 25th. During the forty-five minute drive to my place from the airport, we updated each other on our current and recent past activities, as friends separated by great distance usually do. But as soon as we entered my little cottage, Mark was anxious to examine the old journal left behind by Horatio P. Tripp. He devoured the words with such enthusiastic interest, as if Horatio had been a long lost relative. I didn't have to worry about this being a boring venture for him; not only was he feeding his hunger for an experience with the supernatural; he seemed to be studying the old journal in a scientific manner which didn't surprise me in the least—that had always been Mark's nature.

We awoke at four the next morning, ate a hearty breakfast, and then set out on our journey to test my theory about the mysterious house. I would not have entrusted anyone else but Mark with this fantastically unbelievable anomaly, and if my theory failed us, I sincerely hoped that he would not be angry with me for bringing him all the way from Tennessee on a wild goose chase. He assured me, however, that this was his way of spending a little vacation time, and that he was glad we could do something like this together, just like the days of our youth, no matter how it turned out. I couldn't disagree.

I parked my Jeep in the grassy ditch completely off the roadway. That darkest part of early morning was past, but the Jeep was still lost in the black shadows cast by a grove of giant dogwoods. The sun had not yet risen, but the first hint of light suggested a glorious, cloudless day. There seemed no point in carrying our rain gear, so we left it behind in the car, but the crisp morning air demanded something more than shirt sleeves. Until the sun came up, hooded sweatshirts would keep us comfortable.

By the time we had hiked the half-mile from the road, the deep purple eastern sky had faded to an orange glow. Not even a whisper of a breeze disturbed the leaves, their various crimson and yellow hues now slowly and cautiously emerging from the night shadows. I kept my eyes focused in the direction of where I knew the clearing to be, not quite yet distinguishable in dawn's shade, all the while verbally pointing for Mark's benefit. As the morning's light increased, and the clearing became visible, my disappointment escalated, as the clearing remained just that—a clearing. No old house. Nothing.

"Sorry to chase you all the way up here for nothing," I told Mark. "Guess we can just head back to my place... figure out something else exciting to fill your vacation."

"Not so fast," Mark replied. "I want to stay here for a while longer."

It was Mark's vacation time we were burning up, so if he wanted to linger for a while and stare at the empty clearing in the woods, I would certainly linger with him. So we settled down, leaning against a couple of oak trees with our legs stretched out on the ground. I had conceded to an unsuccessful mission. Convinced that we were wasting our time here, I pulled the drawstring of my hooded sweatshirt a little tighter about my neck against the chill of that October morning, folded my arms across my chest and closed my eyes.

I'm not absolutely sure how long I napped, but as I drifted toward consciousness, I felt the warmth of the sun on my face, and then something unknown abruptly yanked me out of my sleep. Beside me, Mark had succumbed to a nap, as well, and he appeared to be fighting off the same energy force that had awakened me. Within a few moments, I had blinked my way to a fully coherent condition, realizing that the temperature had risen many degrees. I untied and loosened the drawstring, and slipped off the hood of my sweatshirt. Mark was awake now, too, rubbing his eyes and yawning. And then I noticed his actions freeze as his astonished gaze focused somewhere in the distance. I, too, followed his awed stare that I immediately determined to be toward the clearing.

"What the..." I murmured.

"Is that what you expected to see here?" Mark said.

There, in the sunlight, as if the warmth of the sun had incubated it into existence, stood a wooden frame structure, all perfectly intact, but the naked, unprotected wood nearly black with age, and slight traces of steam rising from the darkened wood shingles of the roof.

I stared unbelievingly for a few moments, and then without speaking a word, Mark rose to his feet, peeled of the sweatshirt, and started toward the miraculous sight.

"Think it's safe to go near it?" I called out to him.

"Why not?" he replied. "It's not radioactive." He stopped and turned back toward me. "Are you coming?" he said with a chuckle. "I thought you wanted to see this."

I *did* want to see this old house, but suddenly, for the moment, my apprehension was in control. Horatio P. Tripp's words came back to haunt me: *Anyone going near that house should beware.*

Mark's words, however, jarred me back into real time: "We were never afraid of old buildings when we were kids... remember?"

"But we're older now," I responded. "We should know better."

"Yeah," Mark said. "We should know better than to pass up something so incredible as *this*."

He was absolutely right. This could be the discovery of the century, and perhaps we only had until sundown to explore that possibility. I sprang to my feet, shed my sweatshirt and caught up to Mark, confident that we were acting as responsible adults.

The house wasn't so large, only filling the thirty-foot clearing. It felt to the touch as old as it looked, dry and crumbling with the rub of a finger. It smelled of age, like the musty, decaying odor from any old, abandoned building, nearly to the point of disgust, but I suddenly felt the urge to have a look inside. Mark was already ascending the steps to the entrance door.

The latch holding the door closed was merely a rusty iron bar slid into an equally rusty loop on the adjacent wall. The rusty hinges moaned a dreadful bawl as the door swung into the unknown.

"Step carefully," Mark told me. "The floorboards are probably rotten and weak."

I had expected as much, but to our amazement, not a single squeak emitted from the very solid puncheon flooring. We stood for a few moments in the square room, unquestionably smaller than the exterior, but still quite large. The only light entering the room spilled in from the open doorway, leaving most every part in shadows. No furnishings graced the room; the only discernible features were numerous doors, apparently the entryways into other chambers. So far, it was clearly understandable why Horatio P. Tripp had called it *the house of many rooms.*

We exchanged curious glances. It wasn't a question of *should we open the doors?* It was a matter of which door we would choose to open first.

"I don't know," I said to Mark softly. "It's your vacation... pick one."

"But this was *your* discovery," Mark said. "*You* pick one."

Perhaps we didn't possess the daring nerve we once enjoyed in our bolder days of youth. While we stood there deciding which door to open first, the old house made the decision for us. One of the doors to our right slowly creaked open, as if inviting us to enter.

We cautiously approached and peered into the murky opening. Mark took the first daring step inside, and I followed. Again, without the aid of any windows to provide light, the room seemed more like a dark, dank cavern. Stepping farther inside, there appeared to be a small opening at the other side where a little light seeped in. Now we were treading on pebbled, hard-packed soil. Mark stooped at the passageway to clear the low ceiling. I followed him into daylight. We were outside once more, but the environment appeared quite differently from the crisp October morning we left at the front door just minutes ago.

Here the surrounding woods was more like a rain forest; the air, hot, and humid. I looked up at the forest's canopy; the sun was feverishly trying to burn through a foggy haze.

"Let's look around," Mark said, and he started walking away. I didn't particularly cherish the thought of being left alone, so I followed.

We hadn't walked far when I noticed the sounds of this forest weren't the usual forest sounds I was accustomed to hearing, but more like the sound effects one might hear at a movie theater running an old *Tarzan* flick. The smell of ferns and mud filled my nostrils.

Mark abruptly halted, cocked his head to one side, listening. Then I heard the noise that had captured his attention. A low-pitched gurgling and hissing seemed to be moving closer.

"It might be wise for us to go back," Mark said, and he quickly turned an about face. He was only a step past me when he viciously grabbed the back of my shirt, dragging me backwards. My line of sight had been focused off in another direction, but now, I, too, saw the creature that made Mark decide this wasn't going to be a pleasant walk in the woods. The greenish-gray reptile stood erect, at least twenty feet tall, its red eyes zeroing in on *me* as its next meal. In one instant as Mark pulled me back, I saw the huge jaws and sharp teeth completely fill my vision; I felt the cold breath blowing from its nostrils as the jaws snapped shut like a trap, catching only the fabric of my shirt pocket.

Lucky for us, we outran the lumbering monster to our escape hatch that was too small for it to enter. We didn't stop until we were twenty feet out from the front door of the old house. Bent over with hands on knees, catching our breath, Mark looked at me and said, "Okay, which door next?"

"What?" I exclaimed. "I was almost lunch for that prehistoric Jurassic Park lizard! And you want to know which door I want to open next!"

"Aw... c'mon, Joe," Mark replied. "Where's your sense of adventure?"

I straightened up, gazed down at my missing shirt pocket. "I think it was in that pocket," I said. "Along with my favorite *Papermate.*"

In a minute or so the graveness of the situation had worn off, and like a couple of school boys we laughed our way back to eagerness for more. When we re-entered the square room with its many doors, another one of them slowly swung open. Mark shrugged his shoulders, grinned, and headed for the open door.

"Hey! Wait for me," I called out to him and hurried to catch up.

This dim room appeared as the inside of a log cabin, slivers of light penetrating cracks in the door at the opposite side.

"If there are giant lizards out there," I said, "I'm not going."

"Dinosaur," Mark said. "That was a dinosaur."

Mark's words forced me to realize that this wasn't an amusement park. We had virtually slipped through a portal into a very real primordial realm, and now, we were about to slip into another. I hoped it would be less challenging.

Mark pulled gently on the wooden door handle; once again we found ourselves outside, but this time the forest appeared more like present times—oaks, hickory, and pines—but it definitely wasn't the same woodland we left at the front door, and it didn't feel any less intimidating than the rain forest had. This didn't stop us, however, from wandering out, although we frequently glanced over our shoulders to make certain the escape route was clear... if an escape became a necessity. An eerie stillness hung in the air like a sloop's sail on a windless day. Not a single bird chirped; no squirrels chattered; it was so quiet I could hear a fly buzzing somewhere near.

What happened next came so suddenly, without warning. A dozen or more heads of glistening black hair and wild black eyes atop nearly naked brown-skinned bodies clad only with loincloth and moccasin leapt from behind bushes about twenty yards to our left. Obviously we were not prepared for hand-to-hand combat with the natives, so our only instinctive reaction carried us on a dead run to the right, with a dozen yelping savages not far behind. We managed to get out of their line of sight just over a knoll long enough to duck into thick underbrush. Lying flat on our bellies we watched the moccasin-clad feet run past, unaware of our hiding position. As soon as we were sure our deception trick was effective, Mark and I scurried back to safety behind the cabin door, and we wasted no time to exit the front door of the house.

"I suppose you're going to ask me which door to open next," I said to Mark once we regained near normal breathing again.

"Well no, actually," he replied. "I'm quite sure the house will make that choice for us."

By late afternoon, we had been, among other things, nearly blown to bits by a dynamite blast during a train robbery executed by none other than the Jesse James gang, narrowly escaped from the crossfire between Union and Confederate soldiers during a bloody Civil War battle, and were almost trampled on a dark night by thundering horse's hooves ridden by a man yelling "The British are coming!" Mark and I had entered all the doors in *the house of many rooms*... except one. Quite certain that the house would evaporate at sundown, and even though it was a bit risky, we couldn't let the last door go uninvestigated. If we didn't make it back to the house in time, we could be trapped in whatever era was behind that last door for a whole year. What an exhilarating challenge! We charged into the square room and patiently waited for the door to swing open.

As a complete change of pace, we entered onto a cobblestone street; where, we did not know. Judging by the attire worn by the people we saw, it was a good guess that we had been jettisoned into Colonial time. A not-so-distant bell tolled, and then we noticed a large group of white-wigged men dressed in formal, long-tailed coats and high buttoned boots entering a brick building across the street.

"Let's go see what's going on," Mark said.

Without considering how absurdly out of place we appeared,

we strolled across the street. Nearly to the doorway where the men had entered, a perky little mixed breed yellow dog pranced up to us, sat on his haunches, and barked once. I studied the dog for a moment while Mark stared.

"Spike?" I said to the dog.

Two barks.

"Spike? Is that you?"

Again, two barks. The mutt stepped closer to me, sat, and held out his right paw. I knelt down and accepted his greeting with a shake.

"What are you doing?" Mark asked.

"This is Spike... Horatio P. Tripp's dog... from the journal," I replied.

"Can't be," Mark said.

"Why not? Tripp said in his journal the dog disappeared during his first visit to the old house... never to be found."

"But it's impossible," Mark insisted.

"Impossible?" I responded. "Of all the incredible, crazy things we've done and seen today? And you're telling me that *this* is impossible?"

"Okay," he conceded. "It's possible." Then Mark headed to the entrance under a sign that said *COURTHOUSE*, and pulled the door half open. "Come on," he said to me. "Let's see what's going on in here."

That seemed to be a cue for Spike; he raced through the open doorway. Mark and I followed, only to see a very irritated assemblage of dignitaries, their meeting interrupted by an enthusiastic, barking dog, making laps around the room and causing utter chaos and confusion.

The speaker, seated at a small table at the front of the assembly jumped to his feet. "Someone! Please! Get a musket and dispatch that bloody mongrel!" Then he turned to us. "And seize those men in the strange clothing at once! They must be conspirators!"

I heard the click of flint, the sizzle of sparks, and a loud pop that indicated to me that someone *did actually have a loaded musket* at hand. Unscathed, Spike ran to me and sat, as if hiding behind my legs. By then, several of the men were coming toward Mark and me, and I was quite sure they weren't intending to invite us to dinner. I scooped up Spike, and Mark led the way out the door. We ran down the street and ducked between two houses, hopeful that our pursuers had given up the chase.

We peered out from the alley. Several of the men still followed, stepping briskly and with purpose, and they all carried long muskets.

Mark looked at his watch. "Sun's going down," he said nervously. "We *must* get back to the house soon."

"But those men are between us and the house," I said.

"Well, put that dog down and follow me. We'll circle 'round behind these houses to get past them."

"But I can't just leave Spike here."

"Then I hope you can run fast carrying a dog! Come on!"

Mark led the way as we ran down an alley past the backside of several houses. As we emerged once again onto the cobblestone street, I heard someone yell, "There they are!" Instantly, a dozen more men were in pursuit. As Mark and I ran toward the house, I glanced at the sun that was just settling down on the horizon. Three loud pops sounded, and three musket balls splintered the wood beside us as we pushed through the door and slammed it shut. Moments later, we tumbled down the front steps. Spike jumped free from my arms, and we all sprawled out on the ground.

"You okay?" I asked Mark.

"I think so," he replied. "You?"

"I'm okay."

We sat with our backs to the house, staring for a moment at the west horizon. All that remained of the sun was its pink reflections in the feathery clouds. I turned abruptly to see only an empty clearing in the woods.

Spike licked my face.

THE
OTHER
END
OF
THE
TUNNEL

.

THE OTHER END OF THE TUNNEL
J.L. Fredrick

ONE

Lightning drenched the pitch black night sky revealing ominous storm clouds for as far as the eye could see, and the crackling thunder thumped out an irregular rhythm of a nearly constant echoing rumble. Shawn Kelly and Steve Allison rambled southward along the sidewalk past the darkened storefronts of the three-block-long business district of Main Street. They weren't window shopping. They weren't on their way to a party. Shawn Kelly and Steve Allison were about to embark on a planned adventure that anyone else in the entire town would have considered an act of pure insanity.

A few blocks south on Main Street, the stark, weather-beaten Hawthorne mansion occupied a half- acre weed-infested lot, projecting a year-round haunting Halloween atmosphere to the encompassing neighborhood. It had been spared the torment of vandals and the cruelty of graffiti artisans over the years as its drab, paintless form stood an unscathed, untouched hideous landmark that no one wanted to go near. Children were taught to stay away from the unknown evil presence, and there seemed to be an invisible barrier protecting it from visitors who were unaware of its uncanny legend.

The legend was based on the two old spinsters, twins, who had occupied the dwelling since long before the turn of the century. Emma and Lizzy Hawthorne were said by some to be Salem witches, who must have migrated here to escape the perils of eminent doom. Some claimed they were devil worshippers, or maybe even the daughters of Satan, himself. The stories went on to include that night in 1947 when the Hawthorne twins both died on the eve of their 100th birthday, and when their bodies were discovered, they were buried in unmarked graves and forgotten.

There were as many variations to the legend as there were storytellers, but all concluded with one non-conflicting fact: the ghosts of Emma and Lizzy Hawthorne were still present in that house. They had been sighted on countless occasions by dozens of prominent citizens—too many to discount the validity of the claims.

To their knowledge, no one had ever set foot inside the old Hawthorne house for nearly two decades, but the tales it spawned were endless and the legends those stories inspired were nothing short of intrigue to Shawn and Steve. Although many people of Westland were convinced the lore was simply the product of wild imagination, Shawn and Steve were convinced otherwise.

Tonight, the conditions were perfect. The approach of a thunderstorm would provide the one element consistent in all the ghostly tales they had ever heard. Every sighting of the Hawthorne ghosts through the third story windows had occurred during late-night thunderstorms, and even they had sensed strange auras in close proximity to the house on many nights like this when they watched in anticipation from across the street in the park. But tonight, they weren't just observing. Tonight they were going in.

At ten o'clock on any other July Friday night in Westland, Main Street would be alive with throngs of youngsters enjoying summer vacation, testing the rules of curfew. But tonight, the intensifying storm had most everyone seeking indoor amusement as Mother Nature spewed out her adversities. Except for the usual flow of traffic, Main Street was nearly deserted.

The rain was just beginning to fall as Shawn and Steve dashed across the park to take shelter in the gazebo next to the rose garden. It would offer them modest protection from the elements while they waited for the right moment, as from there they had a clear view of Main Street in both directions, and a clear view of their object of obsession.

Just across the street stood the decrepit, abandoned Hawthorne house. It reeked of neglect, and even during daylight hours, it levied an eerie presence on the surrounding area, but everyone in the town had learned to ignore it—everyone, that is, except Shawn Kelly and Steve Allison. Their burning desire to explore its interior and to discover its mysterious past was more than just teen-aged mischief. It was curiosity beyond all imagination.

What a grand place it must have once been, but more than twenty years of vacancy and neglect had washed away its elegance. Now the Hawthorne house was the property of the State, as the Hawthorne sisters had left behind no known heirs to their legacy. It was only a matter of time before the old domicile would be toppled from its foundation to make way for the ever-increasing progress of the sixties. No one seemed too concerned about its preservation, but rather, all of Westland looked forward to the day when a more attractive, modern adornment would take its place.

Shawn and Steve were no different from any other youngsters in the community: they clearly remembered the instructions they had received long ago to keep their distance from the house, which they had respectfully heeded most all of their seventeen years... until now. They had never been any closer than the iron gate at the entrance to the front yard, that, for as long as they could remember had always been the snarly, unsightly entanglement of vines and weeds. And until just a couple of days ago when they hid the crow bar in the weeds along the fence next to the railroad tracks, they had never ventured to the back side where they were about to make their approach to gain entrance. All the ground floor windows and the only door on that side of the house were boarded up tightly, but just to the right of the barricaded door was an angled trap door at ground level, the entrance into the cellar, unmistakably their way in. And because there were no street lights to illuminate the back yard, the darkness would veil their presence there. No one would ever notice the disturbed trap door somewhat concealed by the tall weeds.

The rain was coming down harder now and flashes of lightning strobed a spectacular magnification of the spookiness across the street. Shawn and Steve sat huddled in the gazebo, staring intensely at the windows on the rounded spire, and the ones just beneath the steeply-pitched roof. But tonight, just like every other night they had repeated this vigil, those windows revealed nothing but total obscurity.

"What do you think we'll really find in there?" Shawn pondered on his imagination of the mysterious chronicle locked up within the walls of the abandoned structure.

"Hard to say," Steve replied. "Probably a lot of old junk. But just remember... we're not going to take anything. We're just going to look."

"Wouldn't it be great to find some proof?"

"Proof of what?"

"That the ghosts are really there."

"Only one problem with that... how would we ever explain to anyone how we discovered it?"

"Good point. Maybe when I'm old and gray I'll write a book

about it."

"Yeah. You can call it "Face to Face With the Ghosts of Westland.""

Shawn wasn't quite sure he wanted to come face to face with someone who had been dead since 1947, but the thought of such an experience was rather entertaining. Scary, but entertaining.

The rain stopped as the thunderheads tumbled off into the northeast, unveiling a crescent moon and twinkling stars playing peek-a-boo among the sporadic, feathery clouds whisking frantically across the black sky. Long, black shadows cast by the lofty oak trees and the huge, eerie house engulfed the back yard all the way to the railroad tracks and beyond. A symphony of cicadas and croaking bullfrogs, accompanied by the whooshing sound of car and truck tires rolling over the rain-drenched Main Street serenaded the night. The storm was over. The thunder was only a distant echo. The third story windows across the street were dark and empty.

The moment Shawn and Steve awaited was at hand. Most of the town was asleep. This was their perfect opportunity.

TWO

Like two cat burglars right out of a bad movie, they hustled into the shadows at the railroad bed. Their black khakis and t-shirts offered little visual exposure from more than twenty feet away. Paranoia sank its teeth into Shawn. Whispering in algebra class was the most serious offense he had ever been caught at. But Steve's boldness was giving him a little added confidence, and he was quite determined to satisfy his curiosity.

Armed with crow bar, flashlights, and two intrepid spirits, they scrambled over the fence. Steve led the way through the brambles, following the same path he had forged just a couple days earlier. They were standing at the threshold of discovery, closer to the scary old building than they ever thought possible. Until now, they had only gazed at the mysterious obscurity from the rose garden shelter across the street. But now, they were about to touch it, and even more incredible, they were going inside it. At last, their imagination was about to translate into reality. And the only obstacle between them and curiosity's satisfaction were a few weather-beaten boards that the pry bar would quickly and easily dislodge.

There was still time to abort the mission. If they didn't make the intended use of the crow bar, they wouldn't have committed any invasive aggression other than trampling down a few weeds. But somehow this didn't seem like an unlawful act; it felt more like a defiant child challenging a parental rule. This was a mission of discovery. They couldn't turn back now, and after all, how much harm could they possibly do?

Steve put the crow bar into action, and half of the portal was quickly laid open. Their flashlights revealed yet another wooden door recessed into the rock foundation wall. That one swung open with ease, exposing the dark, damp, stale-smelling, dirt-floored dungeon. Never had Steve or Shawn stepped so cautiously, while their lights busily scanned the mostly empty space. Only a couple of wood-staved barrels and several old trunks sat in a corner. There were thick, rock walls separating the cellar into rooms, but they were there more for support of the huge structure above than they were intended as partitions. As Shawn peeked around the end of one of the walls, his light found a steep, ladder-like stairway that led up to a rectangular opening in the ceiling.

At the top of the ladder was another trap door. The hinges rendered an eerie, screeching moan as Steve pushed the door open and ascended into a small, windowless room. Shawn wasn't about to be left alone, and was instantly at Steve's side, standing in what appeared to be a pantry, adjacent to the kitchen, and they knew they were at the rear side of the house by the boarded-up window they could see through the doorway.

Gingerly they stepped out of the pantry and into the kitchen, wondering if they would be greeted by the ghosts of Lizzy and Emma Hawthorne. But there was not a sound, or even a hint of motion anywhere.

Under a crusty blanket of dust and a thicket of cobwebs, it was obvious no cuisine had been served up from this kitchen in many years. Rust was consuming the cast iron cook stove, as well as the tin pots and pans on the cupboard shelves. A calendar hanging on one wall still proclaimed the preservation of the last known habitation: July, 1947.

An archway was distinctly the passage into the next room, which was no more than a short, wide corridor, its walls lined with shelves from floor to ceiling, and every one packed end to end with books. So much dust, soot, and mildew covered the spines it was impossible to interpret any of the titles. Shawn's temptation to pull some of them off the shelf for closer inspection was difficult to resist, but he recalled the oath they agreed to before the invasion, "not to touch or disturb anything inside the house." Perhaps another time he would have the opportunity to peruse the archaic library, but not tonight.

Yellowed, moth-eaten lace curtains dangled across the filthy window panes that permitted little or no inward vision, but they did allow the luminescence of the street lamps to dimly light the interior of the front parlor. Shawn and Steve switched off their flashlights as they entered. As if stepping into another world, the grandeur of past extravagance was almost breath-taking. If one could overlook the dust and the cobwebs, ignore the peeling and sagging of the once exquisite rose-colored floral wall paper, and disregard the tarnish on the many brass and silver adornments, the imagination could almost bring the past back to life.

Steve walked cautiously to the center of the room among this realm of antiquity. The air was musty-smelling and deathly quiet. As if time had stood still for the past twenty years, the inside of the house looked as though it had not been disturbed in all that time. Everything was left just as it was in 1947: the upright player piano, the hurricane oil lamps, the elaborate crystal chandelier, the huge oak dining table, the Boston rockers next to the rusty pot belly stove—like they were waiting for someone to return after a long vacation.

Shawn aimed his flashlight at some framed pictures gracing the wall to get a better look. In the dim light it was impossible to make out any of them, but Shawn was compelled to see.

"Shawn!" Steve whispered, as if anyone else was there to hear him. "Aren't you afraid someone out there will see that light?"

Shawn already had the situation sized up. "Take a look at those windows. They're so dirty it's no wonder we've never seen anything from out there. And no one is going to see us, either... and why are you whispering?"

Steve gazed at the windows. They were quite dirty. He could barely see the cars passing on Main Street.

As Shawn made his way around the room eyeing each piece of art, he recognized many of them from the American Literature class he had just aced. Nearly all were signed Currier and Ives prints. But the last one he came to sent a chill down Shawn's spine. He beckoned Steve to take a look. The brown-tinted daguerreotype was of two not-so-attractive women in flowing white gowns with leg-of-mutton sleeves. Their piercing glare seemed almost inhuman.

"Do you suppose these are our two ghosts?" Shawn was certain the picture was of Emma and Lizzy Hawthorne.

Steve stared at the photograph for a few seconds. "Man! They were ugly."

Hidden from their view before, they were now standing at the foot of a stairway leading up into the mysterious darkness of the second floor. But who would go first? Side by side, with each squeaky step, they focused on the black hole at the top of the stairs. As they approached the top, their flashlight beams began to reveal their position, and exposed a familiar fixture. They were at the south end of the building; to their right was the interior of the rounded tower at the front corner facing the park. But what was this regulation-sized billiard table doing here?

Their attention converged on the spire windows. They realized their dangerously close proximity and quickly doused their lights. With due precautions, slowly and deliberately they crept each to one side of the opening and peeked around the edge of the sill to the street below, just as Jake, the City Police Chief was passing by in the squad car. The powerful cowl-mounted spotlight was scanning the empty park across the street. He certainly hadn't noticed the presence of human form in the second story windows on this side of the street. If he had, he was ignoring it completely. The police car continued its slow pace down the road and disappeared out of sight.

The two stood there for a few minutes enjoying the bird's eye view of the city, commenting that "the view from the third floor would be even better."   But first, they had a pool table to examine, and the remainder of the second level to explore.

And a fine table it was. Better than they had ever seen. The coin-operated, six-foot versions at the Bowling Alley couldn't compare to the quality and craftsmanship of this one. It was built of solid mahogany. The slate playing surface was covered with the traditional green felt, but the rails were leather, and all the pockets were real leather, not plastic.

Shawn finally violated the oath. He plucked several balls from a corner pocket. "What's this? All the balls are red. How can you play pool when all the balls are the same color?"

Steve chuckled. "Snooker." He knew the game, but hadn't played it much. "There are fifteen red balls, and if you check the side pockets, you'll probably find six colored ones."

Shawn had to look. Sure enough, six various colors, and numbered one through six.

Steve continued with his brief synopsis. "I don't remember all the rules, but you hafta sink a red ball and then you can shoot at the numbered balls, in numerical order, and sink them only in the side pockets, so you gotta be good at bank shots. You keep score with points for the numbered balls you get in."

Shawn seemed a little baffled. "Okay, Snooker Man... but what were a couple of little old ladies doing with a pool table... upstairs?"

Steve shrugged his shoulders. "Guess they didn't have room for it downstairs in the parlor."

It was time to move on. Looking down the long, narrow hallway running the entire length of the house, they could see one doorway on the left, and two on the right. All three rooms were furnished much the same: large brass beds with feather-filled mattresses, corner chairs, round-topped steamer trunks, ball-footed tables, oil lamps, and pastel-colored chamber sets.

At the far end of the corridor, they found the staircase to the third story. Although this was where the Hawthorne ghosts were always spotted, by now, bold curiosity by far surpassed trepidation as Shawn and Steve ascended these steps with ardent expectations. This was to be the pinnacle of the quest; if anything sensational remained to be discovered, it would be there on the infamous third floor.

The possibility of an actual encounter with supernatural entities still lurked in their subconscious, and the closer they came to that last step, the boldness began to melt away. But unwilling to yield to the gripping suspense of what awaited them, they pressed on, slowly.

THREE

The entire third floor was one enormous open room. With their backs toward the wall facing the street, Steve and Shawn made a hasty scan of the vast space. There were no windows to the back or either end, and the walls had no covering—just bare, unfinished boards. It had the appearance of any typical dreary attic. But there was furniture, graceful and ornate, neatly arranged as if this had once been a primary dwelling. Except for the player piano and the rosy wall paper, this was almost a duplicate copy of the downstairs parlor. The pot belly stove was of a smaller version, and there was no chandelier, and the dining table wasn't quite so large, but everything else was nearly the same. And beyond all this, toward the back wall stood two brass beds with thick, soft-looking mattresses, a night table between them, and chamber pots on either side.

But why was it so dark? Why weren't the street lamps casting at least a little light into the room? It became clearly understandable as they turned to investigate the front windows. It was also understandable why they could not have seen anything, living or otherwise, in these windows from their spot in the park. Dark-colored, opaque canvass-like fabric draped each one, allowing not even an infinitesimal sliver of illumination to trickle in. If no light was getting in, then no light would pass outward, either. Steve experimented holding the curtain to one side. A flood of light poured in. Replacing it snuffed the room into total darkness again.

"I think it might be safe to light some of these candles. No one outside will see them, and we'll be able to take a better look around."

Shawn gave it some thought, and concluded it seemed to be a good idea. "You got any matches?"

By the time Shawn had voiced his approval, Steve already had one candle lit. It was short and fat and its own solidified pool of drippings had it securely stuck to the bottom of a round-handled tin cup. Its flame emitted an eerie, flickering yellow radiance that sent a giant shadow of Steve's silhouette dancing on the wall behind him. There were half-burned candles everywhere. Within minutes they had most of the chamber well-lit, and now it all seemed to be in a little better perspective. But just like the rest of the house, this room had not been host to any mortal stir for quite some time, either, as dust and cobwebs dominated the decor. There was hardly any clutter, and it did seem odd there were no remnants left behind of a past generation, no discarded or forgotten personal possessions that might help consummate the saga of the Hawthornes, or at least cast a little understanding of the lifestyle exercised by the dwellers here so long ago. Shawn kept hoping to find, perhaps, a diary, or a journal, or some recorded memoirs, as he forced open each less-than-cooperative drawer of the old mahogany desk. But the compartments produced little of anything—a couple of quill pens, a dried-out ink well, and three unused candles.

Under the usual layer of dust, in a corner beside a Boston rocker, a small stack of newspapers aroused Steve's attention. They were yellowed and brittle with age. He plucked the top one from the stack, shook away the dust, and read the bold headline:

SOVIETS LAUNCH SPUTNIK II

It was a copy of the State Journal dated Monday, November 4, 1957. And the next one especially caught his eye. The bolder-than-bold inscription at the top of the front page jumped out:

BRAVO, BRAVES

MILWAUKEE GOES WILD

He scanned the first few lines of the epitaph from Friday, October 11, 1957, characterizing that city's reaction to their baseball team's glorious success in the World Series.

"Shawn! Come here. Look at this."

At first glance Shawn exhibited an air of disappointment. "They're just some old newspapers." He didn't immediately recognize the gravity of Steve's find.

"Look at the dates," Steve urged. "Notice anything strange about them?"

Shawn picked up the remaining two editions from the floor and began to read aloud the headlines and dates. "Reds Launch First Artificial Satellite, Saturday, October fifth, nineteen fifty-seven." He flipped to the second paper he was holding. "Braves Do It. Aaron's Homer in the Eleventh Wins Pennant, Tuesday, September twenty-fourth, nineteen fifty-seven." Then it hit him.

"NINETEEN FIFTY-SEVEN!"

"Exactly," Steve confirmed. "If the Hawthorne twins died in 1947, and if it's true no one lived here after that, then how did these papers get here?"

Someone had been in the house a decade after the Hawthorne double demise. The papers were testimony to that. Had the long-departed siblings re-visited their earthly domain? Or, was there some other explanation yet to be uncovered? This was justification enough to suspend the oath and to mount an intensified probe. Not a single corner, nook, or cranny was to go unscrutinized; if there was anything else to find, they were going to find it.

After nearly the entire expanse had been searched inch by inch, nothing more than a few pieces of worthless jewelry had been found. Shawn was standing on a short stool investigating the top shelves of an empty cupboard when he noticed Steve tugging open the drawers of the desk. "I've already looked in there. Didn't find anything."

"But did you pull out the false bottom in the lower drawer on the right?"

"What false bottom?" Shawn almost fell off the stool as he responded to Steve's inquiry.

Steve's sharp eye had noticed that the interior of this drawer was not as deep as the outside, and the exposed bottom seemed to be loose. He pulled a jackknife out of his pocket, stabbed the pointed blade into the soft wood, and carefully lifted out the facade. There, in the hidden compartment, was a two-inch-deep, eight-inch-square cedar box with tarnished brass corners and hinges. Steve hoisted it up onto the desktop. It was heavy. Shawn watched with enthusiastic eyes. They cautiously lifted the hinged top, as if they expected a spring-loaded boxing glove to come flying out. Shawn's heightened anticipation dropped like a rock off a cliff. The box was filled with coins. Just coins. His intellect was expecting something else.

But Steve realized they had uncovered something more than

just a batch of loose change. He recognized some of the pieces as similar coinage he had once seen under lock and key at a museum. He positioned a couple of lit candles for better light, and began removing the coins, inspecting them one by one. They weren't the typical, familiar nickels, dimes, and quarters that would be dropped into the slot of a 1965 candy bar vending machine, or plunked down on the counter in exchange for a banana spit at the drug store soda fountain. There were gold twenty- dollar double eagles, ten-dollar eagles, gold dollars, silver dollars, tiny half dimes, bronze two-cent pieces, silver three-cent pieces, strange-looking nickels and over-sized pennies. There were many familiar dimes and quarters too, but not one of the coins in the entire lot bore a date later than 1887. Steve studied the last coin from the box with intensity. It was gold, with the head of an Indian princess on one side, and the words "3 Dollars" surrounded by a wreath on the other. He had never seen the likes of it, much less, ever heard of such a denomination used as common legal tender, although it appeared quite authentic. His T-shirt served well as a polishing cloth, and he soon had the face of the coin emitting a glistening golden luster.

Even though the box of coins didn't answer any questions, what an extraordinary bonanza this was. At face value, there had to be at least two hundred dollars, but to a serious collector, they were probably worth ten times that amount. But how could two teenagers ever explain their procurement of such a rare and valuable stash? They'd be sentenced to Wales Boys' School, for sure, if the truth ever surfaced. And what about their self-administered oath? On the other hand, they were the only ones to know it had been broken, and they couldn't possibly leave this king's ransom behind.

The wooden box would be too cumbersome to manage, and much too conspicuous, should anyone see them leaving the premises. Thank goodness, pants come with pockets.

The entire house had been explored, and there was probably

nothing more to find. All the candles were extinguished with the certainty that not a single spark remained.

They had entered the lodge of a past society almost two hours ago as innocent, curious, adventure-seeking boys. And now, just after midnight, they were leaving as ravaging thieves. But Shawn justified their actions by saying "You can't steal something from ghosts." Their daring act warranted a reward, and this was it.

As Steve ducked out of sight descending the cellar ladder, he commented to Shawn. "Y' know? We just saw something no one else in this whole town has ever seen. Too bad we can't tell anyone."

FOUR

The exploration wasn't over; they had just barely begun. Standing shoulder to shoulder at the base of the steps, they shined their flashlight beacons around the forlorn underground cavern, taking note of the stone-walled maze standing before them.

"Which way did we come in?" Shawn had led the way to this spot on the way in, but he wasn't exactly sure, right now, which direction would take them back to the exit.

"I think it's this way" Steve said as he headed around the end of one of the barriers. At the far end of that wall was a dead end, but ten feet to the left, their lights found the doorway. Expecting to breathe in some fresh air, Steve pulled open the door, but instead of the stone steps up to the trap door they had pried open, they were staring into a dark hole. The passageway descended with more rock steps that disappeared around a curve. This definitely wasn't the way out, but as long as they were there for the purpose of discovery, they couldn't just walk away.

"It probably just leads to a storm sewer."

"But why would the basement of a house be connected to a storm sewer?"

Shawn recalled a bit of history. "There were hideaways all over Wisconsin for escaped southern slaves during the Civil War. Maybe this is one of them."

The stairs snaked back and forth, as it descended into the cool, damp reaches of the earth. Shawn lost his footing on the wet, slippery steps, and like a bowler picking up a seven-ten split, Steve tumbled down with him. Fortunately, they were near the bottom; the injuries didn't seem too serious. Steve's right knee was bruised, and the underside of Shawn's left forearm was skinned from the awkward landing, but neither was bleeding, and it didn't seem necessary to abandon the mission for such a minor incident. Time would heal their wounds, and they may not ever get another opportunity like this again.

The passageway went on and on, twisting and turning around, under, and over layers of bedrock. As if it had supported frequent travel at one time, the walking surface was smooth and hard-packed, so it was nearly effortless to maintain a brisk pace, just to keep warm in the chilly air. In some places, the corridor opened up wide enough to drive a Mack truck through, and some stretches were barely adequate for Shawn and Steve to walk side-by-side. After walking over an hour, the temperature suddenly seemed to be rising quickly. It was a logical conclusion they were approaching the end of the tunnel, and they would soon be out in the open, warmer air again. About a hundred feet ahead they could see a faint light. As they slowed their pace, suspicious of what might await them there, a startling hum erupted, and a hazy bluish-green glow engulfed them. Stopped in their tracks by bewilderment, they stood there for ten seconds, looking over the walls and ceiling trying to detect the apparatus responsible for the bizarre circumstances. But they saw nothing. Then, like race horses out of the gate, they quickly stepped forward a few feet. The hum stopped and they were standing in total darkness. Their flashlights were dead.

Shawn whispered "What do you suppose that was?" He was too intrigued to be scared.

"I don't know," Steve replied. "But let's get outa here."

Hoping the path was as smooth and clear ahead, as it had been the rest of the way, they cautiously hiked toward the dim illumination.

On the outside, the entrance was encompassed by huge sandstone boulders, completely concealing it from view in any direction. Steve climbed up onto one of them, and Shawn followed. A bright, glowing full moon was the source of the guiding light. But that didn't seem possible. Three hours earlier, when they entered the old house, the moon was just a sliver.

And where had the tunnel taken them? All they could tell was that they were in a valley, with a steep, heavily wooded hillside behind them, and a gurgling stream below the rocks where they sat. They had experienced enough excitement for one night, and as long as they were supposed to be on a camping trip, as they often did during the summer, this seemed a likely spot to get comfortable and sleep until sunrise. They'd figure out where they were then.

FiVE

In the soft, hazy sunlight that drifted to their campsite through a canopy of oak, maple, and walnut, an angry, chattering red squirrel was obviously upset with the invasion of his territory by the two strangers who had taken up overnight residency beside the creek. He darted about through the branches of the majestic timber, and the scolding ruckus was so noisy, it woke Steve from a sound, comfortable slumber. He sat up, took inventory of his senses, and realized that Shawn who had been asleep beside him was not there now.

"Good morning, Snooker man." Steve heard Shawn's voice, but he didn't see Shawn. Still a little groggy, he rubbed his eyes and looked around some more. His disorientation diminished, and he was slowly making a re-entry into reality.

"I was beginning to wonder if you were ever gonna wake up."

This time, Steve honed in on the voice. Shawn was perched high atop one of the colossal sandstone boulders just behind him. He had awoken a half hour earlier and decided not to disturb his campmate, scaled the huge rock, and was sitting there enjoying the solitude of this splendid utopia.

Steve pulled off his T-shirt, knelt at the edge of the stream with his knees on a flat rock that was partially submerged in the water so clear he could see the sandy creek bottom. He cupped his hands and scooped up a refreshing splash of the cool water onto his face. It felt so good, he did it again. The water seemed so clean; he didn't hesitate to quench his thirst at the same time.

Using the T-shirt as a towel, he wiped his face dry, and joined Shawn on the broad, flat-topped rock. From up there, they had a panoramic view of the bucolic glen. The jutting hillside blocked their sight, but the valley seemed to widen off to the north, and in the other direction, the entire valley disappeared around a bend. A dozen head of cattle grazed contentedly in the lowland meadow, and beyond them, a lavish, green forest covered the abrupt slope on the other side.

"Have you figured out where we are?" Steve was just now beginning to give it some serious thought as he recalled their peculiar arrival.

"Nope." Shawn's eyes followed the placid stream winding across the valley floor, hoping to jog his memory of a recognizable fishing hole. This place did seem oddly familiar, but he couldn't make a connection. Perhaps they were just viewing the area from a different angle they had never seen before, and that's why it appeared so alien to them.

Thinking back to the night before, Steve recalled the tumble they had taken on the slippery steps, and he suddenly realized his knee didn't hurt any more. He slid his pant leg up exposing the knee. There was no bruise. Shawn hadn't thought about it until now, but when he inspected his arm that was skinned in the fall, there was no sign of an injury whatsoever. The bulky weight of all those old coins still present in their pockets certainly proved they had not dreamed the previous night's activities, yet, here they were, in a place they couldn't identify, and it was within walking distance from the streets of their own hometown.

As they sat there discussing their options of which direction to start hiking, the sound of some kind of machinery began echoing through the hills. Clink... clink... clink... clink... clink... clink... clink. The sound wasn't familiar. A few seconds later, another noise rang out, acutely overwhelming the first. But this one was recognizable. It was the sound of a circular saw blade singing through a slab of wood. Shawn knew that sound from his Dad's lumber yard.

"I think it's coming from over there." Steve was pointing to where the valley widened behind the sheer bluff.

"Then that's the way we'll go. There's bound to be a road that will take us somewhere we know."

The trail led along the banks of the stream for a distance, then turned abruptly uphill into the woods and followed the contour of the hillside. The sound of the screaming saw was getting louder, but the dense forest kept the source out of their sight. After crossing a broad ravine, the terrain took them to a slightly higher elevation, and just barely visible through the trees, they could see the roof of a building. As they neared the edge of the tree line, the establishment came into plain view, and in the silence between the passes of the saw, they could hear voices, and what sounded like a waterfall.

The unpainted, wood-framed structure stood on a high bank next to the stream, and just behind it was a large pond, as if the water had been dammed. A fifteen-foot-high water wheel was spinning at a remarkable speed as a channel of water fed from the surface of the pond poured onto the top of it. Below the wheel, the water dumped out into another pool, where it re-joined the natural flow of the creek.

Along side the building, opposite the pond, hundreds of huge logs lay scattered about. Four men were rolling one of the logs onto a ramp leading into a large opening in one side of the shed-like structure, while two others were stacking freshly cut boards on a four-wheeled wagon.

Shawn wanted to get a closer look. He led the way as they sauntered down the gradual slope to a more broadside view of the mill. But what they saw as they approached the front of the building stopped them dead in their tracks, speechless. Above the door, in bold black letters, they read the hand-painted sign: KELLY LOGGING & LUMBER CO.

Shawn had seen the old photographs of his grandfather's sawmill in Jasper Valley—the sawmill that his great grandfather built—the sawmill that evolved through three generations of Kelly proprietorship into the prosperous business now occupying a half block of prime real-estate on Main Street. And this was a pretty good replica. But why hadn't he ever heard any mention of the reproduction? And why didn't he know about this place that looked so much like Jasper Valley?

As they scanned the surrounding hills, and gazed up the winding ravine leading away from the mill, Shawn and Steve began to recognize the geographical exactness this valley bore to resemble their beloved recreational getaway. It didn't seem possible, but this was Jasper Valley. Without the dam. Without the lake.

In the past, raging springtime floods came gushing down this canyon, threatening, destroying, and sometimes killing. There was no defense, in those days, against the fury and devastation when the floodwaters swallowed up everything in its path, and unrelentingly forced hundreds of inhabitants to seek higher ground, leaving behind their homes and farms to be buried in muck, or even swept away.

Then, in 1957, the construction began, and two years later the Jasper Valley Dam put an end to the terror. The mighty earthen barrier formed a basin capable of containing the worst deluge, and by 1961, a calm and mellow fifty acre lake nestled between the bluffs that granted a matchless rustic seclusion from the rest of the world.

"You boys lookin' fer work?" The grizzly-looking character startled Shawn and Steve as they gawked at the small clearing where a paved parking lot should be. They hadn't noticed him approaching. He was a giant of a man with a voice to match, dressed in faded, worn bib overalls and a shirt badly in need of a trip to the laundry room. A brown straw hat shaded his unshaven face that wasn't smiling as he looked the boys up and down.

"N-no... we're just passing by... heading back to town." Intimidated by the big man, Shawn was reluctant to say any more.

"Well, okay... but if you change your mind, we sure could use a couple more hands out here. Just go talk to Mr. Kelly. You'll find him at the railroad yard in Westland. Tell him 'John' sent ya. He'll put ya to work first thing tomorrow."

"Okay, John... we'll think about it." Steve tugged at Shawn's shirt sleeve as he responded to John's instructions. He was urging Shawn to make a graceful exit, and he certainly wasn't interested in rolling logs or stacking boards.

Confused—and maybe a bit frightened—Shawn stopped midway up the ravine. "This is all just too weird. That guy just told us to go see my Dad for a job. Why hasn't Dad ever told me about the mill? And where the hell is the lake? And where the hell is the road? It should be RIGHT HERE!" A bit of hysteria was creeping into his speech.

Steve put his ever-comforting hand on Shawn's shoulder,

who definitely needed some calming down. "Hey! Settle down, okay? I'm sure there's a logical explanation for all this, and we're going to get it. Now let's get hiking back to town so we can find out what's going on."

They followed the dirt wagon trail as it wound through the rolling countryside around corn fields and small patches of woodland, up toward the ridge where Highway 28 would be buzzing with traffic. With feelings like being lost in a foreign land, they tried to deter their thoughts of the inexplicable predicament by talking about some of their favorite topics, but it was difficult to ignore the surroundings that had so drastically changed in such a short time. It was only a hundred yards to the familiar railroad grade. At last. Something that hadn't changed—something that was still as they knew it.

Six

The pounding hooves of four chestnut drays pulling a wagon loaded down with the neatly stacked, rough-sawed lumber from the mysterious mill slowed, and came to rest as the driver pressed his foot against the brake lever, pulled back on the reigns, and spoke to his obedient team in a deep, gentle, commanding voice: "Whoooa, Gypsy, whoa." When he was certain the beasts were stilled, he turned to Shawn and Steve. "This here load's goin' to the railroad yard in town fer curin.' Climb up on back... you can ride the rest of the way... that is, if you're goin' to Westland."

It wasn't exactly the ride they were expecting, but this encounter with John didn't seem quite so intimidating, and it was a long walk into town. So they graciously embraced the offer and scrambled aboard. John talked to the four powerful animals as if he were talking to his children, and with a jerky start, the load was soon rolling at speed again. Not only was he a sawyer, he was a skillful teamster, too.

As the horses cautiously stepped over the train tracks, John expertly guided the huge, wooden-spoked wagon wheels up the stone ramps looming the rails. It was a jolting ride for Shawn and Steve sitting atop the lumber, but they weren't concerned about that. Their attention was drawn to Highway 28. There were no cars. There were no trucks. There was no pavement. Just a rut-infested, bumpy, dirt road—if it could be called a road. The topography looked about right, but this sure wasn't the highway that was here yesterday.

Their eyes were glued in the direction they would soon see the familiar sights of their hometown. Off in the distance, over the treetops, the church steeple came into view, and now they knew it was just a matter of minutes before they would be sitting at the drug store soda fountain sipping a malted milk and plotting the weekend activities. That's where they usually were on Saturday mornings, and today wouldn't be any different, despite the unusual experiences so far.

As the freight wagon jostled along the rough road, Shawn wondered what his father would have to say about the sawmill he had kept a secret all this time. And he wondered where this unknown road would lead into town. The later question was answered quickly. John turned the wagon across the railroad tracks, and down a short grade, and then rumbled over a narrow, plank-topped bridge. A row of catslide houses lined the left side of the road, and a jagged ditch paralleled on the right. He knew where they were, and so did Steve. This was Black Creek Avenue and just ahead it connected to Main Street, a few blocks from downtown Westland.

This was Westland, but certainly not the city as they knew it. Many of the building shapes were recognizable, but there was so much missing. The knoll off on the left where the water tower should be was now home to an unpainted wood shack and a flock of chickens. The Pure Oil Gas Station was gone, and in place of the big, stately homes that once graced either side of this end of

Main Street, was a sparse scattering of shanties and little log cabins.

The unpaved streets were heavily populated with more horses and mules than Steve and Shawn had ever seen in one place—even at the County Fair—hitched to buckboards, buggies, drummers' wagons, and carriages of all shapes and sizes. They sat speechless in awe while they watched their strangely transformed town pass by, and the many unfamiliar faces waving to John as he rolled the lumber load down the street, headed for the railroad yard.

John's gentle but stern command to the leaders broke their trance. "Haw, Gypsy, haw." The wagon slowed and began turning left toward a small shack with stacks of boards and timbers all around it, and next to the driveway was a sign that read "KELLY LOGGING & LUMBER CO." The boys had a suspicion they weren't going to meet Shawn's father here, and decided this was a good place to disembark the transport, before they were confronted by someone they didn't want to meet.

This was unbelievable. Not twelve hours ago they had walked this very sidewalk on their way to the park. It was concrete then, but now it was wooden boards they were treading over as they passed by store windows with signs hand-painted on the glass. One read: "COBBLER—BOOTBLACK." Another said "CHANDLER—TALLOWS & LAMPS," and the store they knew as Flander's Hardware displayed a large sign on the front naming it "WESTLAND EMPORIUM." Across the dusty street was the "CLOVER LEAF GENERAL STORE," a barber pole and sign reading "HAIRCUT—10 CENTS," and another small window simply said "SEAMSTRESS."

"Okay... where are all the cameras?" Steve said calmly.

"What cameras?" Shawn asked curiously.

"Well, we must have wondered onto the set for The Wild, Wild West... or maybe Bonanza."

"That's ridiculous."

"Not any more ridiculous than us standing here in a town

84

that looks more like Dodge City than it does Westland."

Outsiders in their own domicile, they were receiving plenty of curious ogles from the townspeople, so it seemed moving on was in order. Steve suggested they should trek toward the north end of the city; his dad's auto repair shop was there, and his house was next-door. Somewhere, there had to be an answer for all this, and maybe they would find it there.

But "Edgar's Service Garage," where Steve's Dad had been a mechanic for the past fifteen years was nowhere to be seen. Neither was his home. Instead of the expected modern, steel structure was a wood-framed barn-like building, and on the front was lettered "GARETT'S BLACKSMITH AND LIVERY," and it, too, was surrounded by more equines, wagons and carriages.

Perplexed, but not out of ideas, Steve said, "Okay... let's go to the rocks. Rocks don't change and they don't disappear."

The rocks—some as big as houses—were one of their favorite childhood spots for play, and more recently, a place of solitude to where they often retreated for privacy. Hidden away in a grove of lofty oaks and pines at the west boundary of the city, those huge rocks had been the site of many cowboy and Indian encounters. They had seen Shawn and Steve through puberty, and adolescence, and their initials were chiseled into the face of one big boulder.

The towering trees they were accustomed to seeing mingled among the rocks were nothing more than saplings and brush. No child's games had been played here, nor were there any inscriptions anywhere. Now the substance of the circumstances was beginning to surface as reality. Suddenly, the works of Lewis Carroll and Jules Verne didn't seem so far-fetched. There weren't any talking animals, or steaming pools of bubbling lava, but it was strange, nonetheless. Today, the security of home had evaporated, as they felt trapped in a pioneer version of the quiet Midwestern community where they grew up. The rocks were the only remnants of familiar recollection, and even this area lacked the comforting tranquility it had once endowed.

Steve climbed up the stair step arrangement of granite to a ledge where they often perched, and Shawn followed. It was a good place to contemplate the predicament, and maybe project a solution.

"I know this sounds crazy..." Shawn was trying not to allow his best friend certify him as a mental case. "But let's consider the facts. The lake is gone; the roads are gone; the water tower is gone; most of Westland is gone. But I don't think all those things disappeared. They just haven't been built yet."

"And we've gone back in time to God knows when." Steve was accepting the concept—as impossible as it seemed—that they had transversed an impenetrable barrier in epic proportions.

"As close as I can figure, this is about 1890. My great-grandfather built that sawmill in Jasper Valley in the late 1880s, and that building didn't look that old... if you know what I mean."

"And I remember when the dam was built. We were in the fourth or fifth grade." Steve counted on his fingers. "That would have been about '57 or '58."

"Yeah... Mom and Dad wouldn't let us go out there to watch... they said it was too dangerous... but we snuck out there on our bikes, anyway."

Steve directed the conversation back to the present situation. "But how did this happen? How did we get here... and how are we going to get out of here again?"

Shawn had already been pondering that thought. "Remember that strange green light in the tunnel last night? When we walked through there is when it happened, and the only way we'll get back to where we belong is to go back through the tunnel."

"What if it doesn't work going the other way?"

"Then I guess we'll have to see John about a job at the sawmill."

By the sun almost directly overhead, they determined it must be about noon, or just a little after. They hadn't eaten anything all day, and they were hungry, so it was decided they would find a way to satisfy their appetites before making the trip back to the valley, the tunnel, and hopefully home.

SEVEN

Downtown Westland, today, didn't have much to offer in the way of restaurants—the popular Bergen's Cafe didn't exist yet, and the bakery wasn't there, either. The pool hall was absent, as was the drug store soda fountain.

In front of the General Store, two elderly, gray-bearded, bib-overalled gentlemen sat on a couple nail kegs, elbows on their knees, and intently studying the checkerboard between them on another keg.

"Excuse me... we're new in town and I was wondering if you could tell us where we might get a bite to eat."

The old gents were so engrossed in their game, they didn't even notice the somewhat out-of-place strangers. "The Hotel over yonder has dern good vittles, but jist so ya know, a helpin' o' chicken stew'll cost ya two bits each."

Steve shaded his eyes from the sun with one hand at his forehead, and pointed to the large sign hanging over the boardwalk just down the block across the street. "Much obliged, sir."

As they headed down the street, Shawn looked at Steve with a quizzical grin. "Much obliged? What possessed you to say that instead of thank you?"

Steve looked straight ahead toward the Hotel and calmly replied, "That's what John Wayne always says in all the westerns."

They walked across the squeaky, bare wood floor of the dining room containing five empty, square tables covered with white linen tablecloths. The walls were lined with the same rose-colored, flowered wall paper as they had seen in the Hawthorne house parlor, and whale oil peg lamps hung from the wall above each table.

A tantalizing aroma of spices, cinnamon mostly, filled the room. It was almost better than the bakery smells they knew from their own time. They pulled the spindle-backed chairs from under the table and sat down just as a heavy-set, middle-aged woman wearing a long, gray and blue calico dress entered from the kitchen.

"You fellers needin' rooms... or are ya here fer the job?"

Steve let his charm pour out. "No, ma'am, we're just powerful hungry. We're here to eat."

"Ya got money?" This princess was not going to win any Miss Congeniality awards any time soon.

"Yes, ma'am... we've got plenty of money."

"Yeah, lookit ya. Fancy store clothes. Guess you ain't no guttersnipe. Today it's chicken stew... and I s'pose ya can already smell the pan-dowdy... just made it. I'll bring it right out."

They didn't know what pan-dowdy was, but if it tasted as good as it smelled, the day wouldn't be lost. And when they had finished the frontier cuisine, they only wished there was more--it was delicious. They each slipped a half dime and a quarter under their plates, and Steve handed two quarters to the woman. "There you are. Four bits. Is that enough?"

"It sure is, and you fellers come back anytime."

As they strolled out the door, Shawn turned back toward the maid. "Much obliged, ma'am."

Out on the street, the horses tied at the hitching posts were jibbing and rearing. They were getting spooked by something. There was a rumbling, and then came two short blasts, one long blast, and another short one. A whistle. A train whistle. People were scurrying to line up alongside the tracks. Rather than the huge diesel locomotives they usually saw rumbling through, Shawn and Steve stood at the front door of the Hotel and watched the not-so-large, black steam engine roll to a squealing stop, billowing a cloud of gray smoke from its stack. In tow behind it were three passenger coaches, a flat car, two box cars, and a caboose.

Like a choreographed ballet, a dozen men and boys began loading and stacking lumber onto the flat, while six others rolled wooden barrels from one of the box cars onto a platform next to the tracks. Passengers filed down the steps at the rear of the coaches and headed to the station house to collect their baggage, and when all were off, departing passengers began boarding. In less than fifteen minutes, the lumber was secured, the box car doors slid shut, and the new passengers were settled in the coaches. The "All Aboard" was yelled out as the conductor leaned off the coach steps waving his arm as a visual signal to the engineer. A silver bell atop the locomotive rang repeatedly as to say "get the hell out of the way—we're rolling." Puffing out even larger quantities of dark smoke, the iron horse slowly started chugging its way out of sight as the spectators waved good-bye to their families and friends on board.

EiGHT

It was a long, hot walk, even taking the short-cut they knew back to the valley under a blistering July sun. The saw was still singing out its mournful cries as the two nomads slipped by along the tree line. They could see John and the others laboring as hard now as they were early that morning. But it was time to put all this behind and not look back. The Nineteenth Century had to stay right where it was, and Shawn and Steve had to return to the security of their own time, to a Westland they knew.

"Our flashlights. They're dead. How are we going to see to get back?" A streak of panic shot through Shawn as he picked up the lights they had left on the rocks at the entrance to the tunnel.

Steve was a little more confident. "The path through there is nice and smooth. We can feel our way along the walls easy enough. We can't get lost. It only goes one way."

After a cool drink from the stream, they built up the courage to start the dreaded, dark journey. They entered the tunnel, leaving behind the setting sun of the past, and in hopes the strange green light would reset the clock to 1965. And they would only know, for sure, when they emerged from the Hawthorne house at the other end.

Just as they expected, the eerie hum commenced and they were soon standing there engulfed in the blue-green haze of the extraordinary phenomenon. And then it stopped. Shawn's flashlight was lit; he had left the switch on. Steve tried his, and that one lit as well. They looked back toward the tunnel entrance. It was dark. Although the one possible escape route appeared to be gone, they thought this was a likely indication they were on their way back home.

Few words were spoken during the brisk walk through the cold passageway, and because they had traveled it once before, it didn't seem as far this time. Recalling the mishap on their last encounter with the wet, slippery stone steps, a little extra caution found them at the top without incident, and at last, they were right back where they started, in the musty cellar seeking the exit among the maze of rock walls.

As they emerged from the broken trap door, the sliver of a crescent moon smiled down at them. They were home.

Their Schwinns, with sleeping bags lashed to the handlebars, were well-hidden and waiting for them in the bushes behind Edgar's. A refreshing swim in the lake, and a peaceful night's sleep on the beach sounded mighty inviting right now, but not before they took a quick tour of the town, just to make sure everything was where it should be. And it was. The cafe was there. The bakery was there. The pool hall. The drug store. Flander's Hardware, and the water tower. And the giant oak and pine trees once again shadowed the the huge rocks where the initials 'S. K.' and 'S. A.' were carved into them. The distant roar of a diesel truck engine and the hum of eighteen tires sang through the still night like music. It was here. It was all here.

At dawn's first light, the two had hardly slept at all. The excitement of such an incredible adventure kept them awake through the night, sitting there on the Jasper Lake beach exchanging comments and observations, ideas and speculations. Their pockets were full of money they couldn't spend, and their heads were full of experiences they couldn't share with anyone else.

As long as they were awake, and the sun was just starting to peek over the treetops, a point of curiosity had to be explored. They were quite certain they would find nothing, but a search of the hill along the near side of the lake would satisfy their need to know that the tunnel, at least this end of it, no longer existed. They walked the shore of the lake all the way to the top of the dam, and far beyond. The terrain had all changed since yesterday as the excavation had altered the contour, and water now covered the creek bank where they had slept the night before. Standing at the crest of the enormous dam, they knew that buried deep beneath it was the mouth of the underground passage.

The excursion had begun on Friday night. All day Saturday had been spent in the other Westland, and for all practical purposes, to Shawn and Steve, this was Sunday. But they were in for one more unexpected discovery. As they rolled their two-wheelers into downtown Westland, it didn't seem like a Sunday at all. The stores were open and conducting business; Main Street was alive with activity. Even the bank had customers coming and going. This certainly couldn't be Sunday.

"There's my usual Saturday morning malted milk connoisseurs. What'll it be today?" Otis asked as they swung open the drugstore door and took their regular stools at the soda fountain counter. Otis Ramsey operated the pharmacy/soda fountain/gift shop establishment for as long as Steve and Shawn could remember, and he concocted the thickest, tastiest malteds this side of the Rocky Mountains. He could almost set his clock by the ritual visits Shawn and Steve made to his ice cream parlor every Saturday morning since they were knee-high to a milk stool.

Otis didn't truly understand the actual reason Shawn asked "Is this really Saturday?"

As if it were just normal chit-chat, he replied "Yup... all day, if it doesn't rain."

"I'll have black cherry."

"Okay... and how about you, Steve?"

"Make mine the same... and can we get them to go?" Steve knew they couldn't talk there, and he was anxious to discuss the time anomaly. The rocks would lend a more confidential backdrop.

The dialogue inspired by their recent encounter endured much longer than the black cherry malts. Now there was a lot more to analyze. They began to realize there was more to this than they first thought, and the longer they talked, the more intrigued they were with pursuing the strange happening. Even though they had spent a whole day at the other end of the tunnel, they returned from the excursion at the same time they had left, and that opened up some speculative possibilities.

"Let's go back there again." Steve was thoroughly convinced it would be safe. They hadn't learned a single thing about the Hawthorne legend, which had been their primary goal. And they wouldn't be missing out on a single minute their planned summertime activities.

Although Shawn had deeper roots in that quantum time zone, he had reservations about making a second journey into it. The possibility of learning something of his ancestry contrary to the admirable tales he grew up with frightened him, and he wasn't too eager to come face to face with his long-deceased great grandfather. They already experienced one close call like

92

that at the railroad yard.

Steve was persistent. "But if we're careful, we don't have to take that chance... and if we go prepared, we can stay as long as we want. When we come back, it'll still be the same time as when we left. We've got plenty of money to use there. If dinner only costs a quarter, with what we've got we could survive a lifetime. I can't think of a better way to go on vacation, and I can't think of a good reason not to go. What'ya say? Let's do it."

After he gave it some thought, Shawn realized it was a monumental opportunity, but app-rehension took precedence over impulse, and he insisted they take plenty of time to prepare adequately for the expedition. A trip to the Public Library seemed necessary, if for no other reason, to learn the meaning of the term "guttersnipe," and why he had nearly been mistaken as being one. If they were going to venture off into a strange land, they at least should learn the language.

NINE

A leap into the fourth dimension might seem like an immeasurable undertaking, even to the most resolute physicist. The theory of a parallel universe actually existing, or another era occupying our biosphere, was just that—theory. To everyone except Shawn Kelly and Steve Allison. But they weren't considering the experience as a scientific break-through that could alter modern man's course of existence. To them, it was an oracle to warden with diligence, for this was the fruit of the many miserable, wet, discouraging nights they had endured in the park shelter, and revealing the secret to anyone else could very well deprive them of relishing the payoff, not to mention that it might land them in the psyche ward. Without a doubt, they would be labed "certifiably loony" if the public got wind of their claim.

Shawn was a notable scholar, so it didn't seem unusual for

him to visit the Public Library, even during summer vacation, to feed his omnivorous hunger for knowledge. Sara Fremont, the gray-haired, pixy-faced librarian had grown to know Shawn well over the past few years as he was the one regular juvenile patron she considered her favorite of all the youngsters to pass through the library doors. They shared a commendable alliance, despite the decades of age difference, as together they had superbly spanned the generation gap utilizing books as their building blocks and compatible personalities as the planks between them.

Sara didn't question Shawn's interest in Nineteenth Century trivia, although she was a bit curious of how he had acquired the need to know that era's usage of the term guttersnipe. And as Shawn sat quietly, paging through a stack of publications, Sara proudly announced she had located a passage to answer his query, and began reading aloud to him. "It says here that guttersnipe was the name given to homeless children, generally orphaned by accidents, illness and savage native attacks. These children roamed and slept in the streets of the cities..."

"Much obliged, Miss Sara." Shawn was practicing the new language. He wasn't going to volunteer a reason for wanting to know, and he desperately hoped she wouldn't ask.

Busy all week with odd jobs and chores around the house and at his Dad's garage, Steve didn't join his adventure companion at the library until Thursday evening. But he did a pretty good job of catch up, and later that night, Shawn filled in all the blanks the best he could.

"Hats," Shawn explained. "That's why people were staring at us so much. We weren't wearing hats. You remember seeing anyone there who didn't have on a hat? One book I read said that in those days people considered themselves only half-dressed if they left home without a hat. And blue jeans were called Kentucky Jeans and Levis have been around since 1850."

Shawn went on for an hour passing as much of the new-found wisdom to Steve as he could remember, and both hoped they had enough information of the time they were about to visit to be able to blend into that society without being too conspicuous. They knew how they would have to dress, and they would recognize many of the terms and expressions in speech, and hopefully, they were well-versed enough with the customs to know how to act if confronted with social endeavors.

Friday night, once again, seemed to be the most appropriate time to begin the journey, but this time they would take with them a few survival items, just in case something went awry, or, if for some reason, the convenience of the General Store became inaccessible. But they would have to be careful in selecting the proper gear. Suspicions would certainly arise by the sight of a nylon pup tent in 1890, so a light-weight portion of canvas and some clothes line rope could suffice as shelter, if need be. Two blankets, a wooden-handled hatchet and a keenly sharpened hunting knife were a must, and a couple of cans of pork and beans, and a pound, or so, of beef jerky would get them by in a pinch. Two extra pairs of socks and long-sleeved flannel shirts for each rounded out the supply list, and all this had to fit into a couple of pillow case-sized denim laundry bags.

All in all, this didn't seem much different from any other camping excursion they had planned, with the exception of where they were headed. They were going so far, yet, so near, and although they were barely leaving their own back yards, they knew little of what to expect. The first sojourn had merely given them a teasing taste, and now they were confident they were ready for the main course. The risk of getting trapped in a time where they didn't belong, or combating the many potential dangers they might face, were of little concern to the two dauntless explorers as they shrewdly continued their preparations to turn back the clock—and the calendar.

As the sun was going down that evening, Shawn and Steve, clad in plain, gray T-shirts, faded, worn Levis, pockets bulging with the bulk of the old coins, work boots, and a couple of old straw hats they found in the Kelly garage loft, sat in the park shelter patiently awaiting the cover of darkness. Now, the sight of the withered old house didn't seem so frightening, but rather, enticingly appealing.

The previous forced entry had not been discovered. The cellar door's loosened hinges were just as they had left them a week ago, so the access this time was effortless and swift.

TEN

They had definitely returned to the same place. The valley was just as serene and picturesque now as it was on the first visit, and this time, two fat red squirrels scolded the intrusion. The creek was still fresh and clean, and the sweet aroma of wildflowers drifted along with the gentle breeze. And just as before, the cry of the saw blade echoed between the hills.

But the sawmill wasn't the same as they had last seen it. Now, there were numerous stacks of sawed lumber, many more logs than before, and another building had been erected, and both it and the mill were painted gray. The operation had broadened, and the changes warranted some scrutiny, but this time from the cover of the woods, as Shawn was still a little skittish about getting too close and being discovered.

There was plenty of time, so a leisurely walk into town with frequent rest stops along the way took most of the morning hours. The arrival back in Westland unveiled more alterations of the town they saw previously. There seemed to be a few more buildings at the town's center, some of the storefront signs had changed, and even some of the trees seemed taller. Quite unlikely, this was just a week later than the first visit. In no way could all these changes and additions been accomplished in a week's time.

"Hey! I 'member you boys... you were here once last summer." The big voice startled Shawn and Steve, just as it had a week ago at the mill. John Aderly came out of the General Store as if he was on a mission. He recognized the boys and paused only long enough to make his acknowledgment of their presence. Then he proceeded across the street where Gypsy and company, hitched to the empty Owensboro freight wagon stood poised and ready for the return trip to the valley sawmill.

"Well," Steve said. "Guess that answers that question. It's a year later than last week."

Some things hadn't changed, though. Horses and mules still appeared to be the principal mode of transportation over the still dirt roads and streets. Hats were still the fashion statement, and the smoke-belching black steam locomotive still rumbled to a squealing stop at mid-day. Kelly Lumber Company still did a land office business, and gray-haired, old gentlemen still played checkers on nail kegs in front of the General Store. And the Hotel still served a mighty fine plateful of chicken stew and apple pan-dowdy for twenty-five cents.

Although several cabins had now been constructed fairly close by, the rocks seemed to be yet untouched, and their seclusion was the perfect spot to stash the tote bags while more exploration was carried out. This might even be where they would call home for a while should the stay get lengthy. Behind those rocks, their campsite would be obscure, and sheltered, and this was the only remaining familiar piece of real-estate that assured Shawn and Steve they were still on home turf.

They already knew what preceded Steve's digs, and his Dad's workplace, so it seemed fitting to make the mile hike west to investigate the beginnings of the Kelly homestead. No more than another dirt wagon trail zigzagged around the fields across the rolling prairie land, a far cry from the straight graveled roadway that would someday cut its path through the countryside.

They stood on a knoll among the knee-high corn gazing toward a virgin meadow where a half dozen Guernsey cows dined on the succulent grass. A hundred yards beyond, white smoke curled into the air from a stone chimney hugging the outside wall of a modest log cabin, and a small barn authoritatively punctuated the vast space.

"How about that, Shawn? You live in a pasture."

"Yeah... well at least I know now what that old rock foundation in the field behind our house is. As small as it is, I'd never have guessed that it was somebody's house."

Off to their right, partially hidden in a grove of pines and cedars, they could see another structure that couldn't be left uninvestigated. This was the location where Shawn had spent a great deal of time when he was a little boy. The tiny, salt box building certainly wasn't the same, but the name above the door sure was: Underwood School. Until its closing in 1957, Shawn had attended his first three years of elementary school right here at Underwood. Now he was beginning to feel a greater sense of connection with the unusual surroundings.

But on the edge of town, not even a rudimental version of Westland High existed. The campus now consisted of another log house, a barn, three haystacks, a corral, and a huge vegetable garden. The football field was a marsh, and the baseball diamond was a pumpkin patch.

The stories they had heard about the Public Library once being the Town Marshall's Office were now confirmed accurate. And although the cosmetics of the entire downtown area were somewhat different now, this Westland was starting to feel more like home. Life seemed uncomplicated here, and if they only had homes to go to, what a great place and time this would be.

Beyond the business district to the south, atop the highest plot of ground in the city, the familiar majestic church steeple towered above the trees, a silent sentry guarding the provincial neighborhood. It seemed to lure Shawn and Steve nearer as the sun settled lower and lower into the western sky. As they walked toward it, they realized this part of their town was less like the Westland they knew. Little development had occurred here yet; where the city park should be, the land was still covered with trees and brush, with a single wagon trail cleared through it leading past the church, over the hill and out onto the open plain. It was hard to imagine the steps of progress that must have taken place to transform this jungle into the active South Main Street where Kelly Lumber Company, the feed mill, the creamery, several warehouses, and scores of homes would eventually rise up.

Only one house and a carriage barn occupied a clearing in the woodland about half way between downtown and the church. It was a grand frontier fortress, proclaiming a certain elegance that seemed misplaced in the proximity of an otherwise rustic settlement. The Romanesque architecture, the gleaming white paint, the sparkling windows, all suggested wealth and success, and would be more appropriately situated on a Southern cotton plantation than here.

Nearly unperceivable in its aboriginal state, Shawn and Steve stared at the noble mansion from the wagon path. Hauntingly familiar to them, the house suddenly took its place in actuality: the shape was right, the placement was right. There was no doubt. This was the Hawthorne house. Not the dilapidated old wreck they had always known; not the spooky, lifeless structure that everyone in 1965 shunned; not the eyesore that many hoped would soon be demolished and forgotten. Rather, it was an eloquent statement of beauty and charm, that, if seen in 1965 would be deserving of notice and reverence, and not the prime target for the demolition wrecking ball.

Across the road, well within the cover of box elder and sumac, Shawn and Steve ducked out of sight to a spot they concluded must be nearly the precise location of the future rose garden gazebo, where in all reality this fantastic journey had begun. There were signs of a previous campsite here: a heap of ashes encircled by a ring of stones, and a couple of logs positioned nearby as makeshift seating. And the Hawthorne house was in plain view across the road. There was enough daylight left to retrieve their gear from the rocks and return to the new found retreat. They couldn't pass up this opportunity to observe firsthand the origin of a legend.

The clothes line rope tightly tied waist-high between two trees and the canvas tarp stretched over it and staked to the ground at the ends was the best shelter they would have for the time being. It would at least keep the dew off their blankets, and barring any hard rain they should be able to stay dry. Steve went in search with the hatchet for a few dry branches, anticipating the desire for a small campfire later on. But when he returned with the armful of firewood, he realized one important commodity had been overlooked when they were packing the supplies.

"Matches," he said in a disgusted tone. "We forgot to bring matches. Guess we won't have a fire tonight."

"That's okay," Shawn said as he dug to the bottom of one of the denim bags. "We can get some at the General Store tomorrow." He pulled out a pair of small binoculars. "But I'm glad I remembered these."

Steve wasn't aware the binoculars had been packed, and expressed he would have rather preferred the matches. But binoculars seemed to be a pretty good idea, too. They would certainly come in handy now.

The tent was fabricated, the unusable firewood was gathered. For all practical purposes, they were settled in as well as they could expect, considering. And although they might have favored a hot, steaming pizza, a can of cold pork and beans and some beef jerky really hit the spot. After all, they were camping.

The brightly painted mansion walls across the road were capturing the last rays of the fiery setting sun as it slowly extinguished the day. The horse-and-wagon traffic had diminished earlier, and now it had ceased entirely. The daily stir was coming to a halt. No street lamps would brighten the metropolis tonight, or for many nights to come. No televisions or hi-fis would be heard from open windows. No roaring diesel trucks slicing through the darkness. No adolescent squealing tires piercing the night. Just as plentiful now as in 1965, singing cicadas and frogs accented the stillness. Westland was retiring for the night. Tomorrow would be soon enough to complete the unfinished tasks of today.

ELEVEN

As dusk drew attention to the oil lamps coming to life inside the manor, two figures, one in a pale pink dress, and the other in blue, emerged through the front door, stood together on the porch for a short time, then descended the steps and strolled toward town. As Steve peered at the young women through the binoculars, Shawn asked "Is it the Hawthorne twins?"

"No. They're too young... and too pretty." Steve recalled the photograph hanging in the old Hawthorne parlor, and according to the stories, if they were accurate, Emma and Lizzy Hawthorne should be about 43 years old now, if they died at age 100 in 1947. These two appeared to be in their early twenties, quite attractive, with shoulder-length blonde hair. They definitely weren't Emma and Lizzy.

As they disappeared out of sight, a third dark-haired girl about the same age, wearing a bright green outfit, and accompanied by a thirty-something gentleman, approached the verandah, and went inside. A few minutes passed, and one of the first pair returned, and not too far behind, the other followed, both arm-in-arm with young men.

Soon after the third couple entered, the honky-tonk sounds of The Flying Trapeze began rolling off the player piano, echoing through the forest. Shawn and Steve watched intently as the images of the waltzing pairs seemed to be having a good time. But Shawn was eyeing the lighted third story windows with more intensity than the parlor affair. Those portals were very dimly lit, and just as in his own time, there didn't seem to be any activity there now, either.

Oh My Darling Clementine wasn't exactly the Beatles or The Beach Boys, but it was a relief from the first tune that had repeated several times. The gala in the parlor continued, and there was still no movement detected on the top floor.

"What ya lookin' at?" That wasn't Shawn's voice. It wasn't Steve's, either. They were so engrossed in the spy session, they hadn't noticed their visitors quietly approach and take up positions just behind them. Startled at first, Shawn and Steve quickly realized these unexpected guests were just a couple of curious kids, and posed no threat. They were friendly and polite, and by now, Steve and Shawn welcomed the contact with other real people, an act they had been avoiding all day.

"Sorry. Didn't mean t' knock ya into a cocked hat like that. Me 'n Brady... we're campin' out by Miller's Pond. We got tired o' fishin'. Weren't catchin' a dad-blamed thing... so we decided to go for a walk. We come here a lot. Didn't 'spect to find other bodies here."

Steve had to quickly invent a reason for his and Shawn's presence. "We're just passin' through. We're from... ah... Saint Louis. We decided to hold up here for a few days... kinda like it here."

"Ya ain't none o' them rowdies, are ya?"

Shawn remembered the term from his research and assured the two fellows that he and Steve were not trouble makers, and were no one to be afraid of.

"What ya need here is a fire. How come ya ain't got a fire goin'?"

"Matches," Steve said. "We don't have any matches. Forgot to get some."

The taller boy dug in his pocket. The grin on his face expressed the pleasure he found in helping out the travelers, and within minutes he had a crackling flame curling bluish gray smoke up into the moonlight.

Barefoot, shirtless, and pants held up with suspenders, he

threw his straw hat on the ground and sat down beside Steve on one of the logs, as did Shawn and the other boy.

"My name is Spencer Garett. My Pa runs the blacksmith and livery over yonder. And this here is my best friend Brady Pendleton. His Pa cuts trees fer Kelly Loggin'. We ain't got a whole lot o' friends. We don't get along too good with the b'hoys, 'n there ain't no other bodies like us around, so we kinda just stick t'gether most o' th' time."

It wasn't difficult to interpret Spencer's oration. He and Brady had separated themselves from the ruffian society because they didn't fit in with that crowd. They didn't seem to be sissies, by any means, but they weren't macho he-men either, and they knew it. But they didn't seem to be ashamed of it, nor did they try to hide it. Their eagerness to befriend Shawn and Steve was genuine and sincere, and was well received.

Because Brady's father worked for Shawn's great grandfather, it was certain Shawn couldn't divulge his real name. He thought of spawning some alias, but that could create problems later, so he hoped just first names would suffice. "I'm Shawn, and this is my best friend, Steve."

They all shook hands like gentlemen, and reclaimed their original seats around the campfire. New alliances had formed instantly, and although Shawn and Steve recognized fifteen-year-old Spencer and fourteen-year-old Brady to be a bit naive, by 1965 standards, and perhaps a little puerile, by any standards, they also saw intelligent, alert, and adventurous new friends.

"Miss Ellie Graham, the school marm, says one more winter o' book learnin' 'n we'll be ready t' go out 'n do whatever we wanna do. We're goin' t' Calyforny t' pan fer gold." Brady's English left some room for improvement, as did Spencer's, but they had a plan and a direction in life. Shawn and Steve were beginning to see more and more similarities of themselves in their new acquaintances, and it seemed almost ironic that, in reality, Spencer and Brady had probably already realized their dreams, many years ago.

The conversation turned to the Hawthorne house when Steve realized the piano serenade had stopped. He described the social event he and Shawn witnessed earlier involving the young ladies.

"Ladies!" Spencer exclaimed. "They ain't no ladies. They're whores! And sure as blazes, that ain't no church social." He went on to spell out the real circumstances.

In years past, the Hawthorne twins had conned everyone into believing they were poor widows, whose husbands had died a gallant death fighting at General Grant's side during the Civil War. They gained the sympathy of the settlement, and earned a handsome living selling themselves to the men folk on the street. But as they aged, Lizzy and Emma had become somewhat undesirable to their patrons, and now their home was a boarding house for younger, more desirable female prostitutes, for a king's share of the profits. Over the past few years, many girls had come and gone, and the ones presently doing business across the road had been imported from Milwaukee, Boston, and New York.

Spencer seemed to have all the facts. "Fer a Half Eagle, a man can stay fer an hour; fer a Eagle, till midnight; fer a Double Eagle, all night, a bath, and breakfast next sun up."

Now it was clear to Shawn and Steve how the Hawthorne twins had become wealthy enough to afford such an elaborate home, and why they had found the box full of money hidden in the attic. And this epic, coming from an indigenous citizen of the time, suggested more logic than the one of Salem Witches, contrived by rumor and imagination of the next century.

Steve wondered how a fifteen-year-old boy could know all this information with any degree of accuracy. "Have you ever been there?"

"Me? I weren't born in th' woods t' be scared by an owl. I wouldn't go near that place, and if ya know what's good fer ya, if ya ain't invited, ya better keep yer distance, too. Them Hawthornes is evil people. They've lived here fer ever, and if ya never seen 'em, they're ugly as coon dogs."

Brady jumped in with his story, too. "Once, I seen a stray mongrel wander into their yard. He lifted his leg t' piss on th' posies. Lizzy was watchin' in the front winder, and as the hound was pissin', he jist keeled over, dead as a barn pole."

Shawn and Steve were agog with all the colorful language their counterparts were spewing out. This was turning out to be an experience far beyond what they had expected, and somehow, they knew it would get even better.

Shawn wanted to learn more about the town and its people, and what better observations could they get than from these two characters? Spencer and Brady had plenty to tell, and the captivating delivery was more than informative. It was downright entertaining.

They told sagas about George Flagg, the Town Marshall, how last year he single-handedly captured a couple of cattle rustlers out at the Duncan ranch, and how once, he shot a road agent right off his horse, and how he had run off the rowdies from Chicago, and just last month, he locked up a drummer for selling bottles of sugar water he claimed to be some "miracle medicine."

The stories went on about the General Store owner, Floyd Donovan, who must have eyes in the back of his head, and Evan Johnson, the proprietor of the Emporium and the best sharp-shooter in Westland. With a '73 Winchester, at fifty yards he could pick a flea off a hen's tail and never ruffle her feathers. Ellie Graham, the school marm at Underwood, had to be the smartest person alive since George Washington.

"And don't be skeered o' ol' Black Wolf. Every Wednesday this ol' Injun comes into town and trades a blanket, or a bead necklace, or sometimes a bone-handled huntin' knife he's made fer a jug o' whiskey at the Gen'ral Store. Floyd's the only storekeep he'll deal with. He ain't never hurt nobody... yet. Ever'body steers clear o' him, and nobody's never heard him speak... nary a single word."

They had no clock to keep track of the time, but it must have been well past midnight. No one had left the Hawthorne house;

there had been no signs of visible activity since the downstairs lamps were put out two hours ago; but the attic was still dimly lit. Spencer and Brady were nearly out of anecdotes, and the supply of firewood had been exhausted for an hour or more, but the prevailing bed of glowing embers created just the right atmosphere for the bonds of friendship to strengthen. Shawn and Steve had made the perfect contact with the time.

Then, through the stillness of the night, the shrill screech of a squeaky door hinge summoned up goose bumps in wholesale proportions on the four boys closely huddled around the dying fire. Their eyes trained on the darkness behind the mansion, where a single lantern revealed two shadowy figures stirring about near the carriage barn. Spencer immediately recognized the nature of the activity: a horse was being harnessed and hitched to a carriage, the carriage that his father had recently repaired, and the equine was the unmistakable 'Cleo,' an off-white Lipizzaner that the Hawthornes acquired from the P. T. Barnum. Cleo was high-spirited but well-mannered, strong but gentle. He was a beautiful beast, but he just didn't measure up to the expectations of a good circus performer. But he handled the gold-pinstriped, cobalt blue phaeton flawlessly as he proudly trotted down the lane from the carriage barn and turned northward into town with the two passengers safely in tow.

"Now where d'ya s'pose them two ol' biddies would be a goin' this time o' night?" And with that question posed but not answered, Spencer and Brady expressed their sincere hopes to meet their new acquaintances again. They bid their farewell and trekked off into the night back to Miller's Pond.

Shawn and Steve settled into the tent and listened for the return of the moonlight riders, as the frogs serenaded them to sleep.

TWELVE

They might have been content with their findings so far, but now Shawn and Steve were drawn into a whole new spectacle of marvel. Spencer and Brady had fueled their desire to discover, and the new esprit de corps could not just be relinquished. A certain social intimacy was established: Spencer and Brady were the direct connection to a society totally obscure from casual visits by the Twentieth Century, and even Shawn and Steve were unsure of the longevity of their access, or if it even existed at all, once they returned to 1965.

With the new day, new inspirations were born, too. The town could now be looked upon with a different perspective. It was almost as if they knew some of the people, from the vivid exposé furnished by Spencer and Brady the night before. Now, many of the faces had names, as well as personalities, and it was easier to understand the dynamics of the lifestyle practiced here. All the books in the Public Library could not have created the realism Shawn and Steve had the opportunity to experience firsthand.

Floyd Donovan was behind the counter with his back to the door as they entered the General Store. "Mornin.' How are you boys today?"

Maybe he really did have eyes in the back of his head. Or maybe he had just simply observed Shawn and Steve through the front window as they approached the entrance.

The interior of the store was poorly lit by 1965 standards. The only light was coming in through the windows on either side of the entrance, and two more on the adjacent wall. The wood-planked floor squeaked as it was walked upon, and the air was saturated with a variety of aromas, ranging from vinegar to freshly ground coffee. Two elderly women browsed near the back wall, and a six-year-old was being coaxed by her older brother to decide on the peppermint sticks or the gum drops. The row of penny candy jars were presenting a tough decision for the tike.

Shawn felt compassion for the children as he knelt beside the little boy. "Here... get some of each" he said as he dropped several pennies into the youngster's cupped hand. The few cents from his plentiful stash was of little consequence, but the cheerful smiles on their little faces were worth a million dollars.

Baskets filled with fresh fruits and vegetables lined the floor of the center isle. Beyond them were several wooden barrels displaying painted labels of Vinegar, Molasses, and Monongahela Whiskey. More kegs were labeled Crackers and Pickles. A pyramid of fifty-pound, cloth sacks of flour leaned into the corner, and on shelves along the outside wall were bottles of Heinz Ketchup, tins of Log Cabin Syrup, and cans of Chase and Sandborn Coffee. There were boxes and bags of salt, spices and sugar. Raisins, Saratoga Chips and pretzels. Peanuts and walnuts still in the shells, baking powder, and Van Camp's canned beans. Plenty of the names and commodities were familiar, but this was far from any supermarket atmosphere.

Steve had just located the boxes of matches when Floyd greeted the two women standing in front of the counter with a small basket filled with their desired items. "Good morning Lizzy... Emma." He was one of the few people who remembered which of the twins had the mole on her chin.

Shawn and Steve froze as they listened to the conversation at the counter.

"Tomorrow is our birthday. All the boarders are away for a few days, and we're having guests for tea."

Floyd proudly announced to his patrons that he had just yesterday received some Oriental tea all the way from the A and P in Milwaukee, but he hadn't picked it up from the railroad station yet. "But if you stop back this afternoon, it'll be here."

The women agreed they must return for a sampling of the special tea, and as they turned to walk away, they nearly collided with Shawn and Steve, who had moved toward the counter to get a closer look. And now they were closer than they really wanted to be, staring into the dark, spine tingling eyes of the less-than-attractive old hags, identical twins except for Lizzy's chin mole. Emma and Lizzy Hawthorne glared at Steve, and then Shawn, as if with the surprise of recognition.

Their jutting, square chins and crooked, pointed noses reminded Steve of Elmira Gulch. Had they worn pointed hats and long, black capes, they could have easily passed for the Wicked Witch of the West, times two. It certainly wasn't difficult to understand why they had become unpopular as ladies of ill fame.

Without speaking a word, all four gathered their composure. Shawn and Steve stepped aside, as Emma and Lizzy hastily disappeared out the front door.

"How much for this box of matches?" Steve asked.

"Ten cents" Floyd replied without hesitation.

As Steve flipped a dime onto the counter, Shawn was taking notice of the July, 1890 calendar tacked on the wall. A black X marked off each day, one through fourteen.

"Much obliged," Steve said. "We'll probably be back for more supplies later."

At least, now they knew it was Tuesday, the fifteenth of July, but they still had no means of telling the exact time. So like a couple of sailors just after pay day, they dodged the horses and wagons on Main Street and headed for Johnson's Emporium.

A Nineteenth Century version of a department store, this one was much brighter inside than the General Store as it had many large windows letting in the sunlight, and boasted a quite cheery environment for the impressive array of goods it displayed. There was everything from Justin's Boots to Winchester rifles and Colt pistols; Stetson hats to pots and pans; currycombs and saddles to orange covered dime novels with titles like Black Beauty, Little Lord Fauntleroy, and Adventures of Huckleberry Finn.

For one of his ten-dollar gold pieces, Steve proudly tied the leather lanyard connecting the shiny, silver-cased pocket watch to his belt loop, and slipped the new watch into his pocket. One more event could be added to the list of reasons this was a special day. This was Steve's first watch. Ever.

They didn't need the watch to know it was getting close to lunch time. Although their lives had been shifted seventy-five years, their stomachs were still on schedule. And today, at the Hotel, they would learn that a beef dodger was a corn meal cake filled with minced beef. Not quite as tasty as the chicken stew, but the apple dumpling for desert was scrumptious.

The train was on schedule, too, making its regular stop on the two day round trip between cities along the Black River and Milwaukee. Nothing seemed out of the ordinary. The steam whistle still frightened the horses, and a crowd still gathered along the tracks, and the usual freight loading and unloading wasn't much different today than yesterday. For Shawn and Steve, the novelty of the steam locomotive had nearly worn off, and there was little here to hold their attention. Instead, their interest was drawn toward the north end of town, where frequent puffs of smoke rolled into the air. Garett's Blacksmith Shop was in that direction and that seemed a likely spot to begin the rest of the day's exploration.

THIRTEEN

Each time Adam Garett pumped the long bellows handles, the hearth fire intensified and the bed of glowing red coals brightened. Frequently, he pulled the horse shoe out of the coals for inspection, and finally he determined it was malleable enough for the nearby anvil and a dozen, or so, shaping blows, followed by a few exacting, gentle taps with the clumsy-looking, heavy hammer. Then, a column of steam rose from the sizzling water bucket as the glowing iron was dipped in, and almost instantly quenched to a cold gray. Adam appeared to know he had an audience, but that didn't slow his pace to check the fit of the new shoe on the huge draft's hoof.

"Gypsy!" Of all the horses in Westland, Steve could identify at least two of them: Cleo, the Hawthorne's white Lipizzaner, and Gypsy, the leader of the Kelly Lumber transport team. Shawn was less impressed with Steve's ability to recognize a horse, and wandered out to where Spencer was splitting firewood. But Steve remained for a few minutes, intrigued by the degree of precision the smithy was demonstrating with the use of only crude tools. Equally amazing was the fact that this very location, in his own time period, was still rendering maintenance for Kelly Lumber vehicles.

Spencer was elated to see his new friends again, but seemed a little disappointed that he would have to spend the rest of the day splitting wood for his father's hearth, and wouldn't have time to socialize.

"That's okay," Steve said eagerly. "You have another ax?" He had split firewood many times, and this would be a good, healthy workout.

Shawn toted the uncut logs from the pile and stacked the split wood against the barn wall as Steve and Spencer kept swinging the double-edged axes, and by four o'clock, Adam was impressed and pleased with three times the hearth fuel he had expected.

Hot and sweaty, the three woodcutters sat in the shade of a soft maple as Brady trotted a bareback dapple gray pony into the yard. He, too, was glad to see Shawn and Steve. "Let's all go skinny dippin' down at Raccoon Holler."

Spencer and Brady had their favorite swimming hole, too, and though Shawn and Steve weren't certain where Raccoon Holler was, going for a swim on a hot July day was common practice, and was particularly welcome after the wood chopping workout.

"Pa? Can I go swimmin' now?"

Adam couldn't say no after the outstanding performance at the woodpile. "Just be home in time fer supper," he told the boy. "And give them other fellers an invite to supper, too. I'll tell yer Ma to fix a little extry." Generous hospitality was Adam's way of showing his gratitude for the labor-intense job Shawn and Steve had helped to complete, and he was proud to show off his wife's good cooking skills.

Spencer bridled a docile mare named Aster, boosted Steve up on her back, and jumped on behind him. Shawn joined Brady on the gray pony, and the four of them rode off into the country to the west.

The swimming hole was a well-hidden wide pool in a stream running through a heavily wooded area that Steve and Shawn only knew as being wide-open farm land, and they had never heard it referred to as Raccoon Holler. The name, and the creek, had obviously dissipated over the years, and what a shame. It was sad to think such a great place was forever lost to greedy land development. But it was here now, and they were going to enjoy it while they still could.

With horses tied to a tree branch, and clothes heaped on the creek bank, the four frolicked in the cool, refreshing water for the better part of an hour, and nearly another hour just sitting on the creek's edge basking in the solitude and allowing the sun and the breeze to dry them off.

Betty Crocker couldn't have served up a finer feast than the fare that came from Mrs. Garett's summer kitchen. Chipped beef and mashed potatoes, Johnny cake and baked beans, corn chowder and plenty of apple cider. No one was going to bed hungry at the Garett's house that night. And even after all the effort exerted on the meal preparation, she didn't seem to slow down much. When the lamps were all lit, and Adam was settled into a big, comfortable chair in the sitting room, Mrs. Garett continued with her never ending chores. Tonight there were shirts to mend.

Adam Garett's home was more luxurious than Shawn and Steve expected it would be. A large, two story frame structure had been added to the tiny, original log house, and although simple in design, the finishing touches delivered a sort of elegance. On this hot July night, Shawn and Steve could only imagine the cozy atmosphere a crackling fire in the huge, stone fireplace would create on a frosty winter day. And the furnishings here were of no less quality than they recalled seeing in the old Hawthorne house. It seemed evident that Adam Garett was a very successful businessman.

FOURTEEN

Dressed in doeskin, shoulder to toe, and a black felt hat adorning his ebony hair tied back in a pony tail, he stood silently in the late afternoon sun with his arms folded around the multi-colored wool blanket clutched to his chest. Black Wolf was right on time. It was Wednesday, and he was in town with his latest creation to barter for the weekly jug of nerve tonic. He looked harmless, but his reputation of being less than sociable was once again affording him a wide berth on the busy street.

"How much d'ya suppose Floyd gets for a jug of his whiskey?" Shawn's question caught Spencer by surprise. Even in 1890 that was not a commodity commonly purchased by a teenager.

"I dunno. About a dollar, I reckon."

Shawn had no intention of buying whiskey. His adventurous spirit was headed in another direction. At least a dozen onlookers gasped in fear and held their breath as Shawn approached the old native and held up two silver dollars. Looking into Black Wolf's eyes, he pointed to the blanket, and then to the coins.

As if they were anticipating something horrible to occur, the spectators started backing away. In the past, Black Wolf had always shunned any contact with the white man, except Floyd, with near violent reactions. No one knew why, but there was no reason to question it, either. And as long as Floyd could successfully broker the goods, many beds would be warmed with Black Wolf's extraordinary blankets.

Shawn's friendly and unafraid expression must have struck harmonious chords. Never witnessed before, a benevolent smile replaced the blank frown on the Indian's seasoned face. He muttered something that sounded to Shawn like "Black Wolf, deal," took the silver dollars, then gently and ceremoniously handed the blanket to its new owner.

Shawn was quite proud of the blanket, and more so the method of acquisition than the blanket itself. No one had ever accomplished such a feat. No one had ever heard him speak. And no one had ever seen Black Wolf crack a smile. No one.

Spencer and Brady would be the guests that night as Shawn and Steve reciprocated the hospitality at their campsite. The meal wouldn't be quite so extravagant, nor the beds quite so comfortable. But all that didn't seem to matter. The fraternity was in focus, and somehow, the beans and beef jerky were the perfect entrées for an open air dinner party around a campfire in the woods.

The soiree in progress across the road, though, was a bit more sophisticated. Shawn and Steve were keeping a close watch on the affair, which was creating high levels of curiosity in Spencer and Brady. They didn't understand how a bunch of old women having a tea party could be so interesting, and there was no simple way to explain to them the complexity of the situation. Even Shawn and Steve did not yet realize the circumstances were about to become even more complicated, as well as eye-popping and hair-raising. Before the night was over, they would have a whole new perspective on the house and the Hawthorne twins.

Seven smartly dressed women had been welcomed in through the front door, and viewing the goings on with the binoculars, this was apparently the birthday tea party Emma and Lizzy had spoken of at the General Store. They could see the old spinsters moving about, catering to their guests with teapots and pastries, and by the looks of things, there was an ample supply of gossip.

As the evening wore on, the tea guests began departing, until only two remained seated, one at either end of the big oak table. One of the sisters was there, too, and soon the other appeared carrying a fresh pot of tea and refilled the guests' cups. One final toast was made as the four ladies raised their cups, and each took long sips.

Nearly simultaneously, the two visitors seemed to gasp, clutching their throats, and just toppled off their chairs and fell to the floor. The twins sat calmly, and continued sipping their tea as if nothing out of the ordinary had happened.

Astonished, Shawn, Steve, Spencer and Brady watched as all but one of the lamps were extinguished. But they could still see inside as the sisters seemed to be concentrating their efforts near the area where one of their guests had fallen to the floor. It looked as though they were wrapping that woman in a blanket, and then they did the same with the other one. It seemed a little unusual that they had waited so long to come to the aid of the ailing women. And it also seemed odd that the two had fallen in a drunken stupor. That last pot must have contained something stronger than tea.

A dim light appeared from the third story windows about the same time the carriage shed door opened, and Cleo was once again being prepared to power a late-night ride.

Although it sounded risky, Steve convinced his comrades to follow as he circled around to a vantage point where they could better view the rear of the house from the railroad track. Something strange was going on, and his curiosity was now at an all-time high.

Just as he suspected, the two women had not just fallen ill. Nearly concealed in darkness, Lizzy and Emma emerged from the back door of the house struggling with one of the lifeless, blanket-wrapped bodies, and with a certain amount of difficulty, they hoisted it onto the floor of the carriage, then disappeared back into the house. Minutes later, the second body was lying with the first. Emma and Lizzy boarded the buggy and Cleo responded to the "giddy-up" command. Steve could only speculate, but he was quite certain the Hawthornes had poisoned their un-suspecting tea guests, for reasons unknown, and now they were disposing of the bodies.

It was apparent now that Westland had not always been the peaceful, crime-free community that Shawn and Steve had always known their entire lifetime. In just a couple of days, they had learned of cattle rustlers, road agents, swindlers, Chicago gangsters, and possibly a trigger-happy Marshall. They had seen evidence of racial discrimination, and the operation of a prostitution house. And now they had witnessed a double murder. Could this really be their Westland?

When Cleo and the carriage had vanished into the night, Brady grew a little nervous with the situation. "We better tell Marshall Flagg about this straight away! I told ya them Hawthornes is evil."

"No," Steve said. "Not yet." He wasn't con-vinced that this was the time to summon the law. After all, the twins could be taking those other women to a doctor. Not likely, but possible. He wanted to be sure of all the facts, and if the theory taking shape in his mind was correct, they may not want to inform the authorities at all. "I think I know where they're going, but we'll never keep up with them on foot."

It kind of felt like sneaking Dad's car without permission as they bridled a couple of horses at the Garett stable. But horses don't have odometers or gas gauges, and Spencer and Brady were skilled bare-back riders.

"How do you know where they're going?" Shawn was curious of Steve's perception, but Steve didn't want to say anything that Spencer and Brady would hear.

"I'll explain later." There wasn't time, right now, to step aside for a private conversation. By now, the Hawthornes had too much of a head start, and Steve wanted to prove his speculation. They mounted the steeds and Steve told Spencer to lead the way to the Kelly saw mill.

Jasper Valley was as serene as it had ever been. Moonlight reflected from the twisting ribbon of water that gurgled along the bottom land, and the still air smelled of fresh sawdust. But tonight it seemed to hold the eeriness of Sleepy Hollow. Never before had Shawn or Steve experienced this kind of apprehension in the place that was always their sanctuary, a natural resort where they could always escape the chaos of everyday frustrations.

Shawn still wasn't sure what Steve was delib-erating as they arrived at the edge of the forest overlooking the mill. But when Steve instructed Spencer and Brady to stay with the horses, as he and Shawn would go the rest of the way on foot, Shawn knew it must have something to do with the tunnel. Now he understood why Steve was keeping the information from the others.

There was no mistaking Cleo. The ghostly white form stood out as the lunar glow bathed the landscape. But no one else, dead or alive, was in the carriage. It stood empty by the creek bank.

Only one narrow opening between the huge boulders would allow access to the tunnel entrance without climbing over. If they took the climbing route, they didn't risk the chance of meeting the Hawthornes on their way out. From atop the rocks, looking down toward the passage entrance, they could make out the shape of a human body wrapped in a blanket, motionless. Still determined to be sure of all the facts, Steve jumped down to confirm the object's identification. It was definitely a human body.

As he rejoined Shawn, Steve began to explain his theory of this bizarre scenario. The tales they had been told about the Hawthorne sisters now seemed to be more fact than legend.

They had faked their own deaths by placing the two bodies of women similar in appearance to themselves in the house, to be found later, somewhat decomposed. In 1947 there wouldn't have been the forensic technology to make positive identification. It would have just been assumed the bodies found in that house were those of Lizzy and Emma Hawthorne.

Shawn had some skepticism. "The Hawthorne bodies were found and buried twenty years ago. Why are we witnessing the act now?"

Steve continued with his theorizing. "We couldn't control the time we arrived here, but maybe the Hawthornes know how to do that. They have come here from a different time. We came from 1965. They came from 1947."

Though this entire ordeal seemed rather staggering in terms of reality, Steve's theory was as valid as the fact that they were in 1890 Westland, and now, almost anything seemed possible. Now it didn't seem so impossible for the Hawthorne twins to appear in that house ten years after their alleged deaths. They weren't dead!

There wasn't any point, now, to try to stop what was already done. Emma and Lizzy would soon return for the second body and right or wrong, the boys had to let history take its unaltered course.

FiFTEEN

Cleo stood like a stone sculpture in the early morning sun, and there was no sign of any other activity in or near the mansion. Steve sat alone watching the sunrise as the others slept, all snuggled under Shawn's newly acquired Indian blanket. With a lot on his mind, he figured he would have some time to himself, and this would be a good time for meditation.

The Hawthornes had committed a near perfect crime. The cadavers would never be found in this time, and when they would be discovered, there would be no reason to suspect they weren't those of Lizzy and Emma Hawthorne, as no one else of that era would be missing. The two women were victims of more than the brutal act of murder. The post-mortem mistaken identity would deny them the dignity of proper burial rituals, and their disappearance would remain a mystery for all eternity.

There was not much Shawn and Steve could do or say without exposing themselves, or revealing the secret of the tunnel. And maybe nothing should be done, considering the impact of altering history. But what and how much could Spencer and Brady be told? Although a close, trusting relationship was established, this was a delicate situation, and somehow, they would have to be kept silent, too. Steve knew he and Shawn had captured the loyalty and admiration of their new friends, so it shouldn't be too difficult to convince them to pledge their allegiance to secrecy.

Steve's concern and the desire to discover the true story behind the Hawthorne legends was building. There were so many unknown facts, and simply speculating was not satisfying his curiosity. The answers were attainable, and he was determined to uncover them.

"The Hawthorne sisters seemed to recognize us at the General Store yesterday," Steve thought over and over. It didn't seem likely that they had ever met before, or that Lizzy and Emma had ever seen them prior to the store meeting... or had they? He and Shawn had been in close proximity to their house on many occasions, and just because they had never sighted the twins, that didn't mean the twins couldn't have observed them watching the house from the rose garden gazebo during the many late night electrical storms.

And if the Hawthornes really were using the corpses of the other two women to fake their own deaths, why were they taking such drastic measures to make everyone in 1947 believe they were dead? Were they running from something, or someone? Why didn't they just disappear? They certainly had access to the best and most secure escape route anywhere on the planet.

Steve was glad to see Shawn stirring before the others awoke. They had a lot to discuss privately, and they needed Spencer and Brady to swear to an oath of secrecy. Steve had a plan for that. He already had a ritual contrived that would be administered, and literally carved in stone, once they moved their campsite to the rocks, which was first on Steve's list of priorities. This campsite was beginning to feel a bit uncomfortable and maybe even less safe now. The rocks would provide more security. If the twins did recognize them, and considering the circumstances that developed over night, this camp was just too close.

Trying to be as ceremonious as he could be, Steve made up the oath of secrecy as he went along, and it seemed to be holding Spencer and Brady in a vigilant state, as he used his hatchet to chisel a large X on the back side of one of the huge boulders, then carefully formed all their initials, one in each section of the X. When he was finished, Spencer and Brady watched with fright in their eyes as Steve held the hatchet toward the sky, and petitioned in a pleading voice to the God, Mr. Firestone, to protect them all against the evils they had witnessed, and to help them keep their lips silent in order to preserve their safety.

Now that it was established that no one would say a word to any living soul about the previous night's incident, Spencer and Brady had to go home to perform their daily chores, but they would return again later that evening.

"Do you think they bought it?" Steve was still a little concerned.

"Oh, they bought it, all right," Shawn replied. "And you! You ought to have your own travelin' medicine show."

There wasn't time for exploration that day. Hours would be spent just discussing what had transpired, and what the next steps to discovery should be. And there was so much to consider.

The Hawthornes had chosen that particular night to commit the deed—their birthday—and that seemed consistent with the stories Shawn and Steve had always heard. That was the main basis for Steve coming to the conclusion they were faking their deaths in 1947. But why were they doing it? Many possibilities existed, but Steve couldn't help thinking it was because they were either wanted by the law, or the lawless. Something, or someone was causing them to create a diversion, and a couple of dead, unidentifiable bodies would do just that. If the legends were anywhere near accurate, and with the distinction the Hawthornes and their house had gained over the years, it was unlikely that anyone would go searching through that house, until two adventurous young boys, in 1965, would be overcome by their inquisitiveness and break in through a cellar entry just to take a look. But the twins hadn't counted on that happening. They had created a ghoulish reputation surrounding the house by allowing themselves to be seen for a while after they were dead, and that should have kept everyone away for all time. Then, by covering the third story windows, they could stay, and move about without being detected in a sanctuary protected by ghostly lore. And because they could not enter or exit by the normal usage of the doors, the tunnel was their only means of coming and going. The construction of the dam and the lake in Jasper Valley in 1957 ended it all.

Shawn and Steve had formulated a workable, conceivable account, considering the first-hand information they had recently accumulated. But the one question of why hadn't been answered yet.

"There's only one way we're ever going to learn the rest of the story." Steve was determined to find the answers, and he knew what they had to do.

"And what way is that?" Shawn was curious, too, but Steve had been three steps ahead of him since yesterday, and so far, Steve's theories seemed quite logical, so there was no reason not to follow his lead.

"We have to go to 1947... through the tunnel."

"But we don't know how to control the time we arrive at the other end."

"We didn't when we came here, but we do now. Last night, when we saw the twins come after the second body, I noticed they weren't in the green light very long... not as long as we were... so I counted the seconds they were in it when they went back. Four seconds. Only four seconds. That must put them into this time in 1947. There's no reason it can't work for us, too."

That fourth dimensional jump would put them into Westland just one year before they were born, so it was a safe bet they wouldn't meet themselves, if their timing was right. But plenty other people they knew would be there, including their parents. Of course, not even their mothers and fathers would recognize them. How could they? They weren't born yet. The only ones who would recognize Shawn and Steve in 1947 were the Hawthorne twins, and they would probably be making themselves scarce, until long after the corpses were discovered.

Emergence from the cellar trap door would be the only risky part of the trip, but if they were careful, no one would detect them exiting the house in the middle of the night. And when they had gained the knowledge they were after, they would simply return to the valley, come through the tunnel light as they had done the very first time, and return home to 1965.

It was a simple plan, and it didn't appear to be any more hazardous than anything they had already experienced.

The sun was dipping below the tree tops when Spencer came running across the clearing behind the rocks. Something was wrong. His expression was one of distress. "Ya can't stay here. Marshall Flagg's gettin' up a posse and they're huntin' fer you!"

"What do ya mean, huntin' us?"

"I heard my Pa and him talkin' today. He even asked me when I last saw ya."

"But why is he lookin' for us?"

122

Spencer caught his breath, and then explained what was happening.

While Shawn and Steve were theorizing, studying, and planning all day, the whole town was buzzing with gossip. Marshall Flagg had turned the crank on the rumor mill when he began asking questions of the citizenry regarding the report of the missing Alice Page and Wilma Kerns. They had not been seen since last night at the Hawthornes' birthday party, and when Flagg's investigation lead to the Hawthorne home, Emma and Lizzy assured him that all their tea guests had left, Alice and Wilma being the last. That's when Lizzy insisted that the two young strangers who were hanging around town must be the ones responsible for the disappearance.

Suddenly, Shawn and Steve were fugitives, and until a method to amend the inequitable allegation was invented, the best plan was to hide. Spencer was convinced the loft in his father's barn would be the safest place, as the Marshall had already looked there. They could hide out there until it was safe to make their get-away once the Marshall believed they had left the territory. Spencer and Brady would sneak food to them, and ensure their temporary refuge would provide the necessary protection.

Two days and nights of camping in the hayloft, unable to get out into the fresh air, not only produced plenty of time to calculate and plan. It also made two very anxious spirits, and by late Saturday afternoon, Shawn and Steve were ready to take their chances on making a run for it.

The Marshall's posse had been unsuccessful in sniffing out victims or suspects. There was not a trace of Alice Page or Wilma Kerns. Never before had a disappearance been so absolute. And now the trail of the only suspects was cold, too, and it appeared as though the intensity of the search was greatly reduced.

Spencer and Brady came to the loft that night with the good news, but with heavy hearts, as well. They knew Shawn and Steve would disappear into the night, never to return. This was

J.L. FREDRICK

going to be a painful parting. The four had shared a brotherhood born of the same doctrine that kept Shawn and Steve always on the same page. Though the companionship was being cut short, the friendships would last forever, and the memories of the past week would live on in each of them for all time.

There wasn't an easy way to just end this brief but special time they had spent together. Steve sensed the sadness gripping Spencer. "Hang on to this, for good luck and to remind you of our friendship." It might have only seemed like a token to Steve, but to Spencer Garett, the five-dollar gold piece Steve put in his hand was the grandest, most meaningful present he had ever received. Although five dollars was a lot of money, Spencer recognized the coin not as a financial windfall, but as the symbolism for which it was intended.

A tear might have trickled down Brady's cheek, but he wiped it away before the others would notice, as Shawn presented him with a Half Eagle, as well, and offered the same "good luck" sentiments. It was a gift Brady Pendleton would treasure always. He, too, saw the memorial of a remarkable fraternity—one that could never be duplicated or equaled.

The horses were bridled and waiting, and now it was dark enough for Spencer and Brady to ride their passing friends safely out of town without being noticed. Knowing they would never see this sight again, as the bare-backed steeds trotted them quietly toward the valley Shawn and Steve glanced over their shoulders to the darkened Westland downtown, and to the silhouette of the church steeple standing tall above the treetops in the moonlight. If their calculations were right, the next time they saw that steeple, more than a half century would have passed, and that steeple would be one of the only remaining sights here now. Spencer and Brady would be old men, hardly the allies they could count on in 1947. That is, unless they were told the secret Shawn and Steve had protected so well all this time.

They had nearly reached the Kelly saw mill where Steve

124

requested to be the point of departure, a destination that had Spencer quite curious. As Shawn and Steve dismounted with their bags of gear, Steve was just about to confidentially confer with Shawn on the subject of arranging a meeting with Spencer and Brady in 1947. But the silence of the night was interrupted by a thunderous pounding of horses' hooves—many horses.

Spencer knew there wasn't time for any lengthy good-byes. "Somebody must've seen us leavin' town, and they're followin' us. Get outa sight in the woods. Me and Brady will ride up the valley and lead 'em off in the other direction so you can get away. Good-bye Steve. Good-bye Shawn, and good luck."

With those words, Spencer Garett and Brady Pendleton vanished into the shadowy hills beyond the saw mill, and Shawn and Steve were barely ducked into the brush at the edge of the dense forest when eight horsemen galloped by just a few feet from where they were crouched out of sight. Hardly visible in the dim moonlight across the valley, Spencer and Brady appeared, and when they knew they had been spotted by the posse, they rode off again with the eight determined horsemen in hot pursuit.

Somehow, Shawn and Steve knew that Spencer and Brady would be okay, and now, thanks to their brave comrades, they had time for a much needed bath in the creek before they started their journey into the next century.

SIXTEEN

"One thousand-one... one thousand-two... one thousand-three... one thousand-four."

Transversing the tunnel, this time, with only the illumination of one candle that wouldn't stay lit if they walked too fast, was more time consuming and tedious than the previous trips had been. The slippery, stone stairway leading to the

Hawthorne cellar was a welcome sight, although they weren't totally certain what awaited them at the top.

As they swung open the heavy wooden door, the stench was nearly overpowering. They had experienced the foul odors of pig sty, dead animals, and garbage dumps, but the magnitude of this far exceeded anything they knew. There was little doubt that the bodies of Wilma Kerns and Alice Page were in that house, and the July heat was performing the intended function. Shawn and Steve were thankful, at that moment, that they were familiar with the location of the exit, and they wasted no time in getting to it. No matter how intense their curiosity, there was to be no investigation of the upper levels of the house on this trip.

The outside air was hot and humid, but breathable, and a relief from the torturous environment they had just passed through. As they sat on the ground in the dark back yard, gasping the fresh air, they suddenly realized they had not taken the planned caution when exiting the trap door, and their exposure to anyone in this place and at this time would not be favorable. The residence surely would soon be in the scrutiny of the authorities, and they didn't want to give anyone a reason to connect them to the event that was already in motion.

As planned, the railroad tracks offered the most subtle route away from the scene. Two blocks from here, a side street led to the eastern edge of town where they could take refuge in the woods at the top of the ski hill. That was the nearest place they were sure of being unchanged that would provide some security, and until they had a chance to scope the town in the daylight, and get a better feel of the new surroundings, it was probably safer to stay out of sight.

Dawn delivered a dreary, dismal day over Westland. But despite the lack of sunshine, the heat and humidity was unmerciful without even a whisper of a breeze.

It seemed a little unusual at first that this still wasn't the city they expected to see. There were definitely signs of development and progress and growth, but not to the degree they had anticipated. This was still a few years before their earliest recollections, and maybe they were just expecting too much.

Several houses flanked the now paved Main Street, and nearly all of the box elders and sumac were gone. The beginnings of a park contained newly planted maples, one small flower bed surrounding a flag pole, and a half-dozen wooden benches.

And just across the street from the park, right where it was supposed to be was the Hawthorne house, less attractive now than the last time they saw it. The paint was peeling and the yard was full of weeds. It was definitely showing signs of neglect.

Very little traffic was moving on the streets—just a few pick ups and small delivery trucks. Westland had grown in size, but it seemed to have regressed in liveliness. It wasn't the usual bee hive of activity. Steve took notice of the vehicle vintage. All the cars and trucks were much older than he thought he would be seeing. Shawn justified that by reminding him that this was just after World War II, and maybe newer cars were still hard to get.

But then Shawn noticed something that didn't quite ring true to him. Kelly Lumber Company was a much lesser version than it should be. The meek little building was in the right location now, but he had always been told that his grandfather expanded the retail business on Main Street considerably by the mid-1940s, and this certainly didn't have the characteristics of considerable expansion.

But this had to be 1947. The dead bodies were in the house. The horrible stench in there couldn't be anything else. All the stories of the Hawthorne twins ended with the certainty of their deaths occurring in 1947. So if this was to be their staged final exit, this had to be 1947.

They sat there on the park bench for a couple of hours, confused, and maybe a little worried about how they might already be responsible for changing the course of history. Could they have unknowingly tampered with the natural order of mankind? Could they have created a forward motion deficiency and sent Westland into being a backward community of poverty? What was life to be like when they returned to 1965? IF they could return to 1965. Guilt was slowly taking command of their feelings, and they were nearly convinced they had plunged their town into doom, without knowing how or why. There had to be a way to put time and legend into proper perspective.

"What ya lookin' at?"

Their near hypnotic condition allowed a young man to approach unnoticed. The silence that had prevailed for at least fifteen minutes while they merely stared across the street at the old house was broken by a voice neither Shawn nor Steve recognized.

"Ah... we were just passin' through... happened to notice that house across the street."

"That's Lizz and Emma Hawthorne's house... quite a place, isn't it? Used to be a lot nicer-lookin' but lately they kinda let it go to hell."

"My name is Steve."

"And I'm Shawn."

"Pleased to meet you, Steve and Shawn. I'm Jesse."

Once again, Shawn and Steve sensed an immediate friendship generating, and right now, the one asset they needed more than anything was a trusted friend in this stranger-than-expected environment.

Steve was interested in learning how deep Jesse's roots grew in Westland. "You lived here all your life?"

"All twenty years of it." Jesse ruffled his already uncombed, short blonde hair, wiped the sweat from his forehead with his sleeve, and unbuttoned his faded denim shirt in an attempt to get a little relief from the heat.

"I live with my grandparents now. My mother died when I was three, and my father was killed in a logging accident about ten years ago, but Mr. Kelly has always made sure I was taken care of. Pop worked for him when he was killed."

In defiance of the infernal heat, a chill went down Shawn's back. Once again, he was glad he had not mentioned a last name, and now it was certain he couldn't. Jesse must have been referring to his grandfather, and although he felt relieved to hear a heart-warming report of his ancestry, he didn't want to hear any more. "So...what do you do here in Westland?" That seemed the most logical question to ask to get the conversation moving in a different direction.

"Well... these days there isn't a whole lot to do here. Lots of people lost everything they had last year when the stock market crashed...some businesses just locked the doors. And I heard that even the bank is in trouble now, so there aren't many jobs to be had. I'm lucky enough to get some work at the depot on the days the train comes through twice a week loading and unloading baggage and freight. Last month, three brand-spankin'-new Model A's came in, and I got to drive them down the ramp off the flat car. Someday I'm gonna buy a Model A. Then I can travel around the country and find me a good job."

Despite his star-crossed childhood, and the seemingly distraught environment he was living in, Jesse still displayed a permanent, natural smile and there was a sparkle in his blue eyes. The plaguing rough times he had just described didn't seem to dampen his spirits, and never before had Shawn or Steve encountered a person with such enthusiastic optimism. Although Spencer Garett and Brady Pendleton were impressively strong in that category, they couldn't compare to Jesse's exceptional attitude and greater intellect.

"So...what d'ya do when you're not working?"

"Grandma and Grandpa have a lot of books, and I read quite a bit."

That was Shawn's foot in the door. "I'll bet there's a whole library in that house over there."

"Yeah... there is. But how did you know that?"

"Oh... just a hunch. What else do you know about that

house?"

Jesse's face revealed a devilish grin as he considered the possibility that Shawn and Steve might be a pair of nomadic desperadoes shrewdly in search of their next target. It wouldn't affect his friendship with them, but it would warrant a suggested realignment of their judgment. "If you're planning on breaking into that house, I'd reconsider if I were you."

"No way. We wouldn't think of doing something like that." Shawn knew that statement was teetering on the threshold of a lie, but he hoped he had been convincing enough to keep Jesse from formulating some adverse opinions regarding their presence in Westland. But now, Jesse had stirred his curiosity even more. He seemed to know more about the Hawthornes and their house, and somehow, Shawn was going to get him to tell the story.

"Have you ever been inside it?"

Jesse didn't appear too shaken by their inquisitiveness, or reluctant to provide the answer, and then some.

"Yeah, I've been inside a few times. Lizz and Emma Hawthorne take a lot of trips to Milwaukee on the train, and when they get home, they pay me fifty cents to haul their baggage back to their house. They always invite me in for a cup of tea when I get there. And when Mr. Capone comes to visit, he pays me five bucks to wash his car in the back yard. He's a millionaire, you know."

Their eyes widened as Shawn and Steve huddled closer, and to be sure they correctly understood Jesse's delivery, they exclaimed in unison, "Capone?"

"Yeah... Capone... Al Capone... you must've heard of him. Everybody's heard of Al Capone."

Shawn and Steve just nodded in acknowledgment with their ears perked to Jesse's every word.

"Mr. Capone and his boys have been visiting the Hawthornes quite regularly," Jesse went on. "I think they stop off on their way to his place up north. They'll get here in the evening, spend the night, then take off again the next day, heading north. They've been doing this for a couple of years now. Lizz and Emma must have something real special going on with Capone. He's always bringing stuff to them. Last spring, a truck pulled up to the door and they unloaded a fancy billiard table. Now, every time Capone and his men come to stay over night you can see them shootin' pool, there, in the upstairs windows.

"But lately, it seems that Capone's visits haven't been so friendly. Something must've happened between them. I think it must have something to do with the girls he brought here to stay with the Hawthornes. They just disappeared. Rumor is that they were prostitutes Capone brought in from out East, New York or Philadelphia. It's kinda strange, too. They were here for a while, and then one day they were just gone, and no one saw them leave, and no one's seen them since. Pretty young things, they were, too.

"Lizz and Emma got on the train for Milwaukee last week. They're usually gone for a week at a time, so I reckon they'll be on the next train day after tomorrow. When I take their bags to the house this time, I'm gonna ask them how much they'd pay me to trim the weeds in their yard, and maybe even repaint the house. It sure could use a coat of paint... and I could sure use the money."

A few sprinkles of rain plummeted from the gloomy sky. There was no doubt a good soaker was needed, but Shawn and Steve were not exactly prepared for that kind of weather now. The makeshift canvas tent wasn't going to provide adequate shelter from the approaching storm.

"I'd invite you to our house for the night, but Grandma doesn't like me to bring friends over, but there's an old hay barn no one uses any more outside of town just out past the church. You can take cover there tonight if this storm amounts to anything, and maybe I'll see you again tomorrow."

As Jesse sprinted away across the park, Shawn and Steve gathered up their totes and headed for the town's center, hoping to find the likes of a grocery store. Their food supply was nearly non-existent.

"Do you suppose we should tell Jesse tomorrow that he won't be cutting weeds or painting the house?"

"Nah... but we should tell him not to drink any more tea at the Hawthornes'"

Shawn, being a well-read history student, was overflowing with a fountain of recalled information. On the way to the abandoned barn, after acquiring cans of pork and beans, sliced peaches, and a loaf of bread from the sparsely stocked store, he began to spell out the facts of their current predication in time.

"This can't be 1947. Considering the condition of everything here, now, Jesse must be talking about the beginning of the Depression when he spoke of "the stock market crash last year." That happened in 1929. So this must be 1930.

"And brand-new Model As? Certainly not a car of 1947. And then there's the part about Al Capone; he was put in Federal prison for tax evasion in 1931, and..."

Shawn paused a few seconds contemplating the validity of Jesse's story. "Do you think he can be talking about the Al Capone? The Chicago gangster?"

Steve shrugged his shoulders. "Sure... why not? How many Al Capones could there possibly be?"

The vacant barn was just where Jesse said it would be. It was nothing more than a shed with one large open door at one end and no windows. A layer of loose, dry hay covered the floor. Not exactly the Hilton, but at least it was a roof over their heads. Now that the rain was beginning to fall more heavily, that old barn suddenly was the Hilton.

Now that they determined what year they had stumbled into—1930 and not 1947—Steve's theory for the purpose of the bodies lying in the Hawthorne house didn't seem to fit into the scheme of things. If the twins were attempting to mock their own deaths, and they allowed the public to see them leaving town on the train, they hadn't done a very good job of covering their tracks. And this was just 1930. It was a well-known fact the Hawthornes would remain in Westland another seventeen years. Surely, this was not the final departure meant to be the flimflam that would remove them from the census. The corpses were bound to be discovered soon, and the Hawthorne sisters would be exonerated of any wrong-doing. History mandated their escape from prosecution, and insured their undeserved freedom.

Though it seemed to be a collision coarse with an impenetrable brick wall, there had to be more pieces of the puzzle yet to be considered. As they drifted off to sleep to the sonata of the rain on the tin roof, the rumbling thunder, and the whistling wind, they were thankful that, at least, 1930 had allowed them an escape from the rigorous pursuit of Marshall Flagg's posse.

SEVENTEEN

He heard the sparrows chirping, and a dog barking somewhere off in the distance long before Steve opened his eyes to yet another gray, overcast day. The rain had stopped sometime during the night, and now the only visible indication of the passing storm was a puddle of water just outside the barn door, rippled by a gentle breeze. Occasionally, a flock of sparrows would gather around the tiny pond like tourists on a beach. They seemed so pleasantly fascinated with the newly created neighborhood pool.

Shawn awoke as Steve handily removed the lids from the canned peaches with his hunting knife. He handed one of the cans to Shawn. "Here. I made breakfast."

They had sufficed with much less on a number of previous camping excursions, so all things considered, these accommodations weren't all that bad. They had kept dry through a thunderstorm, slept quite comfortably on a soft bed of hay, and now they were dining on sliced cling peaches. They couldn't expect much better than this.

"You know," Shawn said, as he slurped down the last peach slice, "if this is the Depression, and with the amount of money we have between us, we would be considered quite wealthy in these times."

Steve contemplated their financial status. "Then I think we should definitely have lunch in the finest restaurant we can find."

"Well, I wouldn't count on finding too many fine restaurants in Westland in 1930."

As it had in the past, and would in the future, the Prairie Lutheran Church steeple towered magnificently above the city. Shawn couldn't help but think, as they hiked past the mighty structure, what a remarkable history that steeple had witnessed over the decades from the days of the pioneers' prairie schooners, to the age of space travel. And although he had only viewed a microscopic portion of it, he was confident that no one else ever had the opportunity to experience Westland's vividly graphic chronicle as he and Steve were doing right now.

Just as yesterday, not many people were moving about. Westland now was a ghost town in comparison to the city Shawn and Steve were accustomed. The only consolation was that they understood the circumstances, and it was comforting to know these conditions would all pass in time, and that their home town would some day be restored to the lively metropolis it was always meant to be. For now, they had to ignore the current ambient factors, and concentrate their efforts on why they were here in the first place. The Hawthorne sisters had created a mystery for them to solve, and they were feeling a desperate need to do just that.

The rest of their theory had fallen apart, but one fact was for sure: the billiard table on the second floor that had puzzled them at the very beginning of this adventure was put there and used by Al Capone, a hero to some, but a murderous gangster to most. Lizzy and Emma Hawthorne had a connection, friendly or otherwise, to one of the most notable figures in American history within the society of illicit activity. That is, if Jesse had his story straight. Shawn and Steve could only assume, at this point, that he did.

It seemed peculiar that the bodies of Alice Page and Wilma Kerns had not yet been discovered, although, during the entire time Shawn and Steve observed the Hawthorne dwelling since their arrival in this era, not a single living creature had even come near it. It appeared as though the invisible barrier that protected it from intruders and vandals throughout the '50s and '60s was already in full effect. Jesse confirmed that the ill-natured social attributes of the Hawthorne sisters must have stemmed back long before the days the legends were born, and long before Emma and Lizzy forevermore parted company with Westland's surviving society. His adamant recommendation to evade confrontation with that particular piece of real-estate corroborated every word of warning Shawn and Steve had ever heard.

By mid afternoon, absolutely nothing had happened across the street, and as the minutes and the hours ticked by, Shawn was beginning to lose his patience. "I say we go over there and look through the windows. Maybe those dead bodies aren't even in there."

Steve wasn't exactly in favor of the peeping Tom plan, and although he didn't think it was a very good one, Shawn did have a point. And in the absence of an active neighborhood, there was little danger of being seen, even in broad daylight. With plenty of experience in stealth approach to that house, they knew the best route was from the railroad, and this time they wouldn't wait for darkness. If they were going to detect anything inside, they would have to make their move before dusk.

EiGHTEEN

They strolled nonchalantly across the yard from the tracks toward the back of the house. The thought of what they would see inside raised goose bumps and made their spines tingle. But now it seemed necessary and they were compelled to learning all the facts, no matter how gruesome the facts were.

Just as Steve was about to peer through the window which he knew would reveal the kitchen, an intrusive distraction cut the attempt short of its goal. The crunching sound of car tires on the gravel driveway, and the purring of an engine pierced through the still afternoon air. Along side the house, the long, black sedan stopped, and as Shawn and Steve peeked around the corner with curious awe, the car doors swung open and four men dressed in dark-colored, pinstriped suits and black hats emerged. One of the men had a white carnation on his lapel. The driver stood guard at the side of the car, as the other three strutted toward the house.

"Wow," Shawn whispered. What kinda car is that?"

"A '29 or '30 Packard, I think." Steve wasn't absolutely certain, but it was a good guess. It surely wasn't a common Ford or Chevy, and these guys weren't door-to-door salesmen.

"Do you suppose that's who I think it is?"

"Shhhh!" Steve heard the vigorous knock on the door and he wanted to hear the conversation between the men that was audible, but not clear enough to understand. There was another rap on the door, and then in a sweet but stern tone, a voice from the porch called out: "Emma? Lizzy? It's me, Al."

There was a quiet pause, and then it sounded as if the door was flung open, and moments later, it slammed shut again. But the men had not entered the house. Their footsteps could be heard on the porch deck, and they were talking but still not loud enough for Steve to make out what they were saying. He heard what sounded like hard-soled shoes clicking down the steps, and then nothing.

It had been totally quiet for a couple of minutes. Steve looked to the black car in the driveway thinking the men must be returning to it. But even the driver who had not accompanied the other three to the door was not at the car now. They had not been paying any attention to him.

It felt like the grip of death that grabbed them from behind, hoisted them up, spun them around, and pinned their backs to the wall all within a split second. It happened so swiftly, they didn't have time to even think about a means of defense or escape. As the two brutes held them there, helplessly suspended with their feet barely touching the ground, the third man—the one with the carnation on his lapel—instructed Karl, the driver, to return to the car, to make sure no one came near it. He stepped up closer to Shawn and Steve. "What are you boys doing here?" he asked, as he struck a match and lit the cigar clenched in his teeth.

Shawn and Steve were so stricken with terror they could not speak, for only inches away, before them stood the one and only Al "Scarface" Capone staring into their eyes. They knew this could very well be the end of their journey. Certainly a villainous character with the unscrupulous reputation he had acquired would think nothing of leaving two more lifeless bodies lying in the back yard of a house in this small town. Was their final thrill in life to be so briefly in the company of this celebrated criminal?

"It's okay, Mr. Capone. They're friends of mine. Don't hurt them. They're okay."

Jesse's rescuing plea came from out of nowhere, and was the sweetest sound Shawn and Steve could have expected. On Capone's signal, the henchmen released their captives, and backed away. Jesse was now poised next to Capone, offering his hand in a friendly gesture of greeting.

"Good to see you, Al. Did you have a nice trip?"

The message to Shawn and Steve in Jesse's eyes was quite clear: "shut up and let me do the talking." He obviously had a stronger relationship with Capone than he had let on before, as the mobster seemed to immediately recognize Jesse, and there was no doubt he trusted the word of the smiling, blond-haired youngster.

"Hello, Jesse," Capone said. "I wired Lizzy last week. Told her we'd be here today to collect. Things were gettin' a little hot in Chicago, anyway. It was a good time to spend a few days at the cottage up north."

Not only did Capone and Jesse have an established affinity with one another, they were on a first name basis. And as long as Jesse maintained a friendly status with them, Shawn and Steve were somewhat confident they would have little to fear of Capone and his boys. They would follow Jesse's lead, and keep quiet.

Jesse began to offer some information. "Lizz and Emma aren't here. They—"

Capone interrupted. "Oh, they're here, all right, but they're laid out on the sitting room floor, dead as a pair of mackerels on a beach. And the inside of the house stinks worse than a morgue run out of ice. Looks like we aren't going to collect today and we won't be doing business here anymore."

Jesse's expression turned to a puzzled frown. It was the first time Shawn and Steve had seen his face without a contented, cheerful smile.

"Does that mean I won't be seeing you any more?" Jesse seemed almost devastated.

"Not unless you come with us right now and work for me. I'm not coming back here. Don't want to get nailed for snuffing out the Hawthornes. This wasn't a very profitable operation, anyhow."

"No," Jesse replied. "Thanks for the offer, but I have to stay here and look after my Grandma and Grandpa. But as soon as I get enough money saved up to buy that Model A, maybe I'll come visit you sometime."

Steve noticed the look of compassion in Capone's eyes.

Shawn was curiously concentrating more on Jesse's oration of intent to continue the association.

Capone leaned toward Jesse, put his hand on Jesse's shoulder, and spoke more quietly, as if to shroud the conversation with a little privacy. "I know you've been saving a long time for that car. How much are you short?"

Without hesitation, Jesse humbly replied with the figure he knew too well. "Three hundred and fifty dollars, but what I make at the depot, it'll be a long time before I have enough."

Al Capone retrieved a bankroll from his pocket and began counting out bills. "Here. Take this. It's enough to get you that Model A, and maybe a little left over."

"But Al... I can't..."

"Take it. It's yours. Just remember... you didn't see me here today, and make damned sure your friends understand they didn't see me, either."

Jesse was either a very good actor, or he sincerely was moved by the developing situation. Shawn wasn't certain which, as Jesse's bewildered grimace lingered.

"Don't be sad, kid. Mark this day as a new beginning. Now I have to get out of here. And give my regards at the funeral."

Capone and his entourage wasted no time to board the limo. Jesse was right there, and made another attempt to inform Al that the Hawthornes would be returning on the next train, but Karl sped away before he could get it all out. Al Capone was gone for good, and by the look on his face, as he watched the black sedan disappear down the street, so was a part of Jesse. His secretive alliance with a man who not many knew the way Jesse did had abruptly come to a bittersweet conclusion.

Shawn and Steve were still overwhelmed with the association between their newfound friend and the Mafia boss, and the chain of events they had just witnessed. This might have defined why Jesse could sustain such a buoyant disposition during such stressful times. He probably had few worries thinking he was within the protective circles of the organization.

But he probably wasn't aware of the dangers that lurked in Capone's shadow. Capone had plenty of enemies, as well, who would gun him down in an instant, along with any near by associates, if the opportunity arose. But this was neither the time nor the place to tell him that.

"Are you guys okay?" Jesse asked as he walked back toward Shawn and Steve. A forced smile replaced the frown, but concern was still in his eyes.

"All things considered," Steve replied, "we're doin' just fine. But what about those dead bodies in the house?"

Jesse wasn't yet convinced the corpses were really there. He had to see for himself, so he jumped up onto the end of the verandah and stepped cautiously to the door, peeking in through the window. Certain that the Hawthorne sisters could not have returned from Milwaukee, he slowly opened the door, stepped part way in across the threshold, peered around the half-opened door, and quickly stepped back, slamming the door shut abruptly behind him. He covered his nose and mouth with one hand, nearly gagging from the repulsive rank fumes. Shawn and Steve had already experienced the putrid foulness, and they had no desire to subject themselves to it a second time. They already knew the bodies were not those of Emma and Lizzy Hawthorne, and there was no point seeing they were really there. Jesse's confirmation of their presence was good enough.

"C'mon, Jesse," Steve urged. "Let's go over to the park and sit down." At the moment the Hawthorne yard didn't seem to be the most favorable spot to contemplate a reasonable course of action, and the park was distant enough to escape the eerie atmosphere suddenly surrounding the residence.

The three of them sat on the park bench, just staring across the street, without speaking at all for several minutes. Jesse was clearly making an attempt to regain his composure. A portion of his world had crumbled and he was mentally searching for a means to heal the wounds he suffered in the destruction. His ties with a long-time friend were severed, and now the Hawthorne twins—one of his sources of income—were dead. Could this day get any worse?

He soon found the resolution within him, and he realized that none of all this really mattered. His pocket was stuffed full of money, the likes of which would have taken many months to earn, providing the railroad kept operating. And the Hawthornes? They were just a couple of old bats who he could survive without. Now, he didn't have to rely on painting their house in order to afford a Model A.

"I'd better find the Constable and tell him about the Hawthornes," Jesse said. "Don't go anywhere. I'll be back in a little while, okay?"

As Jesse started to walk away, Steve was compelled to give him one bit of information. "But that's not the Hawthornes in the house."

Jesse looked over his shoulder as he kept walking on his mission to make the report to the only peace officer in town. "Who else could it be?" He, along with Capone, had fallen for the deception. The Hawthornes really had faked their own deaths, but not for the reason Steve had theorized right from the beginning. The twins would return, and the question of why they had choreographed this elaborate production was still a mystery.

NiNETEEN

Like three pigeons perched on a window sill, Steve, Shawn and Jesse watched from the park bench as a small, curious crowd gathered in front of the house. The Constable's brown '28 Chevrolet coupe, Dr. Butler's '27 Lincoln, and the undertaker's black panel truck, all parked in the driveway, had drawn considerable attention, but the throng of people quickly began to disperse as two men with towels wrapped around their faces carried the first corpse out on a stretcher, and the disgusting odor drifted to where they were gathered. By the time the second cadaver was being loaded into the panel, no one remained. Even Doc Butler had left as there was nothing more he could do.

As the undertaker drove away, Constable Wade Sheppard spotted Jesse, and started walking toward the park. He was half way when Steve quietly commented on the remarkable resemblance the Constable had to "Paladin." Only Shawn made the connection. The popular television western series "Have Gun-Will Travel" would not entertain home audiences for nearly another thirty years. Puzzled, Jesse asked "Who's Paladin?"

Sheppard approached, and spoke to Jesse. "Well, the Doc declared them dead, all right. Any dern fool could've told me that. But them gals aren't Lizzy and Emma Hawthorne. They must've been some boarders living upstairs. Don't know who they are… or should I say… were."

Jesse perked up. "Then they will be on the next train."

"Yup," Sheppard replied. "If you saw them get on the train last week like you said, they'll be back tomorrow. I can't imagine they'll take too kindly to their roomers dying in their parlor and stinking up the place like that. You better warn them when they arrive. You'll be the first one to see them. Tell them to come see me before they go home from the depot."

Eager to oblige, Jesse responded to the Constable's request. "Yes, sir. I'll tell them."

Sheppard started back across the street to his car, but only a few steps into the journey he stopped, turned back toward the boys, and posed an after-thought question to Jesse. "By the way, you haven't seen that Capone fellow hanging around lately, have you?"

"No sir. Haven't seen him lately."

One of Shawn's curiosities was answered. Jesse was a good actor.

After Sheppard was well out of sight, Shawn initiated the quest for more answers that only Jesse could provide.

"Just how well do you know Al Capone?"

That's all it took to get Jesse talking. Now that Capone was gone, there wasn't any reason to keep his past coalition a secret any longer, especially to the fellows he now considered his new pals.

"Al took a likin' to me the very first time we met a couple years ago. He came into town late one night. Lost, I think. He asked me if I knew where Lizz Hawthorne lived. Well, next thing I knew, I was riding in his car giving Karl directions to the house. When we got there, he said to me, "you're all right, kid," and he stuffed a greenback in my shirt pocket. I didn't know who he was then, but I've been invited to the Hawthornes every time he's come to visit ever since. He taught me to shoot pool, and how to win at poker. I could never beat him, but never once did he ever take my money. He always gave it back when the game was over.

"Then, last year, just before he went to jail out East, he brought these girls here, and another truck followed him in that time, too. Guess it was supposed to look like the girls were moving in, and I guess they were. But most of the boxes and trunks were full of liquor. I know because I helped tote it all into the cellar. Al paid me real good that night.

"Lizz and Emma have been selling that bootleg on the sly, and I reckon they were taking in quite a haul on the girls, too. And then while Al was in jail, the girls just disappeared. No one saw them leave, and no one's seen them since. Lizz had just come back on the train from Milwaukee. As usual, I hauled her bags to the house, and as usual, she invited me in for some tea, a special blend she'd picked up at the A 'n P in Milwaukee. While I was sitting at the table in the kitchen waiting for the tea to brew, the girls went down into the cellar, and they never came back up as long as I was there. I never saw them again after that.

"There were a lot of people who weren't real happy with the Hawthornes about that time. Most everyone knew what was going on there, but when word got out that it was Al Capone supplying the liquor and the women, no one dared do anything about it. I guess they were all scared of Al, and they just turned their heads the other way when he came to town. Of course, there were those who were regular customers, too, and they probably didn't care where the stuff was coming from.

"When Al finally came back, he was pretty upset to find out the girls were gone, and I don't think he's ever forgotten about that. But the liquor and beer kept coming for a long time, on credit I suspect, and he must not have gotten his payments, 'cause he cut them off a month ago. He looked kind of mad today when he thought the twins were dead. S'pose he figured he wouldn't ever get his money. That's why he said he wasn't coming back here again."

Shawn saw the sadness in Jesse's eyes reappear as he spoke of Capone's absence. "But Jesse. You know who Al Capone really is, don't you?"

"I know you think he's a really bad son-of-a-bitch, and yes, I've heard all the stories about the stuff that's going on in Chicago these days. But Al never did anything bad to me. In fact, he always treated me real good, like a big brother, and I'll miss him."

The sun had gone down since Jesse began the saga, and now the frosted round globe street lamps dotted Main Street with blotches of soft glow. Shawn and Steve had hardly spoken a word while they soaked up every syllable of the extraordinary testament. This was a piece of Westland's history that was obviously little-known, and rarely, if ever spoken. It was amazing that a famous figure like Capone could have left his distinct imprint on this city, and the pages of time simply wiped it away, leaving not a trace for posterity.

They all bid their good-byes. Jesse had a busy day at the railroad station head of him. Steve and Shawn had a long night of mystery solving awaiting them at the barn where they could discuss the day's events and Jesse's declamation in unconditional privacy.

TWENTY

The cryptographic conundrum scattered and entangled throughout decades of time was finally deciphering itself. The long trail of unnoticed clues was now being noticed, and strangely making sense. Jesse had filled in the blanks, and he made it understandably clear how and why certain events occurred. Now there were fairly substantial facts to start rewriting the Hawthorne legend.

In the seclusion of that little barn, way into the wee hours of the morning, Shawn and Steve reconstructed the time line paralleling the Hawthornes.

"They probably learned the finer points of running a prostitution business from Capone..." Steve began. "They took that know-how back to the 1800s. Their connection with him explains a lot of other things, too. They suckered him out of a bunch of money, which by 1890 standards made them filthy rich. No wonder they could afford that fabulous mansion back then."

Shawn recalled part of Jesse's story. "The girls we saw that night in 1890 were actually the women Capone brought to the Hawthorne house in 1929. Jesse said they disappeared into the cellar and never came back. That's how they vanished without anyone seeing them leave town.

"When Lizzy and Emma had conned Capone out of as much as they were going to get, they planned the fake death ordeal just for Capone's deception. They knew he was coming to see them today. He sent them a telegram a week ago. They knew when to put the dead bodies in the house, knowing it would be him to find them. They left town on the train so everyone else here knew they weren't around when the others kicked off, and just like the Constable said, he didn't know who they were, probably just a couple of boarders. Didn't sound like he was even too concerned.

"And you know no one will go into that house snooping around. Not the way that place stinks. Bet they planned that, too."

The Hawthornes had acquired a bundle of cash, and now they were rid of Capone and clear of the murders they committed. Now that the bodies of Alice Page and Wilma Kerns were used as decoys to ward off Capone in 1930, then perhaps Emma and Lizzy actually did show up as the guests of honor at their own funeral in 1947. If that were the case, then it wasn't they who had revisited the mansion ten years later leaving behind the 1957 issues of the newspaper. Someone had, but who?

"The only others who had any knowledge of the tunnel were the girls," Shawn said. "Maybe it was them."

"What do you mean?" Steve asked.

"Maybe it was those girls who returned to the attic. After the twins died, the girls could have gone back there frequently, and easily ventured out into the town without being recognized after so many years."

"Do you think the ghosts everybody saw was them and not the Hawthornes?"

"It's possible. I can't think of any better solution."

The diabolical probabilities were calculated to a reasonably logical conclusion. It didn't really matter how the Hawthorne sisters managed to elude blame for the deaths of the other two women, but the story still didn't seem to be complete. Once again, a visit to 1947 was necessary.

TWENTY-ONE

The northbound train was just pulling out from the station. Only six passengers had disembarked, and now, only two of them remained on the platform next to the depot. Lizzy and Emma Hawthorne, in long, black dresses stood there watching as Jesse rolled their luggage toward them on a steel-wheeled cart. It rumbled across the planks, and came to rest beside them. Shawn and Steve couldn't hear the conversation, but the content of Jesse's speech was evident by the expressions and body language. The twins' reaction of surprise seemed a bit artificial, but Jesse was buying it. And just as he was instructed to do, he pointed them in the direction of the police station. He would keep their bags until they returned, quite certain that this time they would be delivered somewhere other than the house.

When it was safe, Shawn and Steve came out of hiding and approached Jesse as he began to load some wooden crates that had come off the train onto another cart. They were there to say "good-bye," and they knew this was going to be another sad moment. Another friend was being left behind—one they would never see again.

"You guys take care," Jesse said. "If ya ever get back this way again, be sure to look me up. I'll take you for a ride in my Model A. Maybe we can tour the whole country together."

The calculation was pretty simple: Four seconds in the strange green light in the tunnel had shot them forty years into 1930. One second for every ten years. So just under two seconds should bring them forward to 1947. One-point- seven seconds, to be exact. There was no means of measuring time that precisely, but it was worth a try. A stop in that year would perhaps supply an accurate final chapter. It still wasn't absolutely certain that the twins didn't attempt another masquerade party then, too.

It was still broad daylight when they carefully pushed the cellar trap door open just far enough to test the safety of making their exit. Leaving the premises now would definitely present a degree of danger. They surely didn't want to be seen.

The candles were getting short, and the musty, damp cellar wasn't going to provide very comfortable quarters while waiting for the sun to go down. The wooden kegs were still where they had been before, and seemed to be the only dry spot to sit. One candle was snuffed out to preserve some duration, if the need arose. A decision had to be made, and maybe if they sat in silence for a while, they could determine if there was any activity on the floor above them. This was the first time they had been within the confines of the spooky old house during daytime hours, and was certainly the most dangerous, without the cover of darkness to guard them from detection by anyone outside... or inside.

They had no way of knowing their arrival in this era was more than a month after the Hawthorne sisters had been laid to rest in a small, private cemetery plot, only a couple miles from the edge of town.

The silence was broken by the sound of nails being hammered into the exterior walls. Not realizing what was going on, Steve's curiosity got the best of him, and he convinced Shawn, as well, they had to investigate. The noise was definitely coming from outside, so they could possibly gain access to the first floor in the obscurity of the pantry.

Steve climbed the steep stairway with Shawn close on his heels. He pushed the trap door open, and the two of them climbed a couple more steps, exposing their heads and shoulders above the level of the pantry floor. A blood-curdling scream from outside startled them, and they quickly ducked below the floor, and pulled the trap door closed over their heads. Motionless, they listened, as they could now hear the hysterical conversation between the two carpenters, just outside the kitchen window.

"I'm telling you! I saw two people in there. It's got to be the ghosts of the Hawthornes. I saw them in there. I know it was them!"

His partner climbed the ladder leaning against the wall beside the window, and peered in through the opening remaining from the lack of one board left to be put in place.

"I don't see anything in there now. Hand me that last board. I'll nail it on. Then let's get the hell out of here!"

Shawn and Steve could hear the hasty hammer strokes and the abrupt ladder removal, and the two men scurrying away, mumbling their intent of never returning to finish the rest of the windows on the other sides of the house.

Now deathly quiet, it was a safe bet there would be no one near the house, and from the carpenter's comment about the Hawthorne ghosts it was clear the house was void of any occupants. They had missed the funeral, but at least it was safe to come out of the cellar, and perhaps seek the security of an upstairs room for the time being.

Their hunger was the only contributing factor that made Shawn and Steve venture out that night. The big, brass-framed feather bed in the second floor bedroom was quite soothing, considering this was the first actual bed they had laid on since their visit to 1890 when they were overnight guests at Spencer's home. Dusk was falling on Westland as they awoke from a well-deserved nap. They could now safely get out of the house in the evening shadows, and hopefully there would be an open eating establishment to satisfy their need for nourishment. Dino's Cafe was only a couple blocks away, and it was always open at night; at least it was in 1965. And it would be interesting to see if the burgers were as tasty now, or if that was an art that had to be developed over the next eighteen years.

Big Band sounds, Glen Miller style, filled the interior of the diner. The source was an antique-looking juke box with a rainbow of colored lights, and a curved glass top displaying the 78's and the primitive turntable apparatus. Dino's was bustling with activity. It was probably the only place in town open for business at this hour. Trying to be inconspicuous, they took seats at the counter, and ordered their burgers.

Eavesdropping on the various conversations around the room became quite entertaining, but the one being conducted right behind them proved to be the most interesting. One of the four men seated at the table was obviously the carpenter who had misidentified Shawn and Steve as the Hawthorne ghosts earlier in the day. He hadn't changed his drastically inaccurate and highly exaggerated account of what he thought he had seen.

"...And there they were, floating up out of the floor. It was them, all right. I saw them with my own eyes. I know I'm not going back there to board up the rest of those windows."

Not to be outdone, one of the other men told his version of a recent experience. "One night last week... that night we had the thunderstorm... I was walking by the house on my way home from the pool hall. I happened to look up just about the time a bolt of lightning lit up everything, and I saw them plain as day in a window up in the third story..."

A third voice from the same table added his opinion. "I knew when they put those two old hags in the ground out on Harper's Hill that they weren't goin to stay there. I just knew the Hawthornes would come back to keep on tormenting the town somehow."

The fourth man had comments, too. "I heard once that a couple of young girls staying at that house disappeared. They never did find them, and then another time, two other women were found dead in there, too."

Shawn and Steve were holding back the chuckles as they finished the burgers. At the moment, the stories seemed pretty hilarious to them, but to the storytellers, this was serious stuff.

They were believing what they wanted to believe, whether it was true or not, and no one was about to alter those misconceptions.

As in any small community, gossip spreads quickly, and this story had made the rounds with record-breaking speed. The carpenter's sighting reinforced the previous rumors with solid-as-granite proof. The earth had rejected those vile creatures, and now, their evil, miserable spirits were lurking still, within the walls of that old mansion. And everyone seemed to agree that if no one ventured near it, the twins would remain there, and could cause no harm.

From all the comments they observed most of the next day while just hanging out on Main Street, the people apparently were quite satisfied it was Lizzy and Emma Hawthorne buried in the graves on Harper's Hill. No one was sympathetic over the deaths of the Hawthornes. There didn't seem to be any fortifying reasons that justified their unpopularity, just trivial complaints, mostly of their unsociable nature, their unwillingness to keep their lawn groomed, and it was the older sector of citizens who remembered that place as a den of immorality. And now that they were dead, they were the talk of the town. Having an honest-to-goodness haunted house right on their own Main Street must have been the biggest news to hit Westland since the end of World War II, and that house was certainly receiving its lion's share of local publicity.

Shawn and Steve didn't know where Harper's Hill was located. They had never heard of it before, but it couldn't be far away, and asking the right questions of the right people should lead them to it.

It was starting to appear that the entire ghost sighting ordeal really was just a hoax. Shawn and Steve, themselves, were the essence for part of the legend's beginnings, when they were spotted coming up out of the cellar. Not totally impossible, someone could have been observed through the upstairs windows, too, but it probably wasn't the Hawthorne twins. Imagination on the part of the observers was definitely playing a role. Exaggeration was filling in the blanks.

For the sake of his own satisfaction, if nothing else, Shawn grew more determined to locate the graves on Harper's Hill. Steve thought it less important, but Shawn finally convinced him that they should seek the obscure little cemetery now.

"If we don't find it now, maybe no one in 1965 will know where Harper's Hill is. The stories all say "they were buried in unmarked graves and forgotten," and now we have the opportunity to find out where those graves are. They shouldn't be too hard to spot. They'll still be kind of fresh. It's only been a month."

"Yeah," Steve agreed. "We did come here to find out everything we can."

Now it was a matter of talking to some of the people on the street. Someone here was surely able to give them the answer they needed.

A mature looking man was just exiting the Bank a half block away. He was the person they would approach in hopes of attaining a rapid answer. As the man neared, Shawn turned as pale as the ghosts they had been chasing. He shifted his body around as the man passed by, so as not to let the man see his face. Steve suddenly realized who the man was: Shawn's Grandfather.

"I was afraid of this," Shawn moaned. "Grandpa Kelly died when I was seven. I was hoping this wasn't going to happen."

Steve knew, and remembered well, Grandpa Kelly, too. And now that he had almost come face-to-face with him, Steve better understood Shawn's apprehension of such an encounter, and he could feel Shawn's anxiety. They had been successful, so far, to avoid contact like this. They would have to be just a little more cautious from now on.

"Excuse me..." Steve said to another gentleman he was certain of not being any relation. "Could you tell us how to get to Harper's Hill?"

The man looked at Steve with a strange stare, and then at

Shawn. "Dyin' would be one way."

That answer was frustration enough, without having to ask again. "No. I mean can you tell us where it's located?"

"Ain't nothin' out there but a graveyard. Why the hell would you want to go there?"

Steve realized now that he had chosen the most obnoxious being on the whole planet, and there probably wasn't any reason to continue the conversation.

They walked down the street a ways, and sought a response from yet another. This man and his wife were pleasant and helpful.

"It's out west of town. Just take the gravel road at the end of the street in front of the Bank. At the first crossroads, go left. It's about a mile from there, but you aren't gonna find anything there any more except a graveyard. It used to be the old Harper place, but even the buildings are all gone now. All that's left is the graveyard where they're all buried, the Harpers and Hawthornes. Lizz and Emma were the last ones left of the whole clan. They were buried out there just a month ago. Shady characters, they were. Bootleggers back in the '20s and '30s..."

"Thank you. Thank you, very much! You've been a big help. We'll be sure to mention you when we write our book."

The gravel road they were told of would take them past the spot where Shawn's father would eventually build his family's home, and the crossroads was just beyond that at Underwood School. That meant that the Hawthornes' graves were not more than a mile as the crow flies from Shawn's house. They had been by that old cemetery hundreds of times, but there was never any reason to pay attention to it.

And in the event the no marker stories were correct, it seemed necessary to visit the site now, so they would know exactly their location.

A two-mile walk in the country proved to be a gratifying change of scenery. Shawn and Steve had grown somewhat accustomed to the slower, less hectic pace of the former

Westland, and now the post-war industrial age was encroaching their city. They had never viewed their modern generation's lifestyle in this way, but now that they had experienced the utter beauty that once surrounded the community, they wondered if all the technology and development and progress was really a fair trade.

They had almost reached Underwood when Shawn remembered a remark Steve made, and quite frequently he was amazed with the lightning-quick replies Steve could produce.

"When we write our book? May I ask how you came up with that?"

"Well, the other night you said you wanted to write a book, and if they can write a story about a house in Kansas getting relocated by a tornado to a place called Oz, then someday, we can write an equally unbelievable story about all this, too."

He did it again. Steve always had an answer.

TWENTY-TWO

The tiny, thirty-by-thirty cemetery, encircled by a split-rail fence, placed there only to keep farm machinery from knocking down the tombstones, contained the poorly maintained grave sites of a dozen or so Harpers and Hawthornes, all of which dated back to the 1800s. It wasn't surprising, now, that if Emma and Lizzy were the last remaining members of the clan, there was no one left to carry out the placement of the traditional, hand-carved family headstones. Only a small heap of field stones rested at one end of each of the two recently dug graves. Weeds were beginning to take over, and it wouldn't be long until those plots would be lost to nature, and forgotten by man. At least one small detail of the Hawthorne legend was accurate.

But right next to the unmarked Hawthorne graves, were two more headstones that did not bear either of the names of the rest. Ragweed hid part of the inscriptions, so Steve stomped it down to get a better look. Both read: UNKNOWN WOMAN— DIED 1930.

To everyone else, these were unknown souls, but to Shawn and Steve, the two people buried in those graves were no mystery. They had names. They were Alice Page and Wilma Kerns.

Shawn and Steve were the last to see them alive. Shawn and Steve witnessed their murders. And now Shawn and Steve were standing over their graves, concurring that it was bad enough the deaths of these two women were the product of greed, but worse yet, they and their families had been deprived the dignity of a proper burial rite.

"At least," Steve said compassionately, "their names should be on the headstones. Let's put them on there."

He had proven his stone carving talents once before with the same hatchet he was still carrying in his tote. Although his style wouldn't necessarily match that of the other markers there, that didn't seem to matter. The important aspect was they were making a sincere gesture to their fellow mankind. It would only take a few minutes, and no one would ever know it was they who had placed the names there.

He was nearly finished when a deep voice called out from behind him. "Hey! What are you boys doing there?"

In this part of the country, horses were still one mode of power for farm work, and their near silent movement across the fields, allowed this farmer to approach unannounced. He didn't look too pleased with Steve's humanitarian act.

"I'm going to go ring up the cops. You can't be hacking up tombstones like that."

Before Steve could get out a response in an attempt to justify his actions, the farmer was well on his way toward a farm house, not too far away.

"Think he'll really call the cops?" Shawn asked.

"I think he looked real mad, and I don't think I'm going to

stick around to find out if he's really got a telephone."

They picked up the pace considerably on the way back into town. Maybe the increase in industrialization did serve one good purpose. There were more places to get lost in the proverbial crowd. But as rapidly as rumors streaked through this town, the time to find a safe place to hide was probably minimal.

An open door on a boxcar near the end of the freight train just beginning to creep away from the down town depot was their invitation to a free ride part way back to Jasper Valley and the tunnel. Timing couldn't have been planned this perfectly. They didn't know if the '46 Ford police car cruising the area at a faster-than-casual rate was in pursuit of them, but at this point, there was no need to take any chances. As they tossed their duffel bags onto the deck of the rail car, two pairs of hands extended from around the corners of the open door, offering the much-needed assistance in climbing on board. It was one of the unwritten ethics of the nomadic drifters—the railroad bums—to help one another in a time of need, and these drifters had also seen the police car, and Shawn and Steve making their evasive maneuvers. It was apparently a time of need.

"Now get outa sight 'til we clear the city limits," one of them said, as Shawn and Steve scrambled to their feet and grabbed their bags, heeding the instructions from the more seasoned rail travelers.

There would only be time for brief introductions, as the new-comers would disembark at the Lake Road crossing just a short distance out of town. They knew this train wouldn't have a full head of steam by that time, and just as inexperienced as they were at jumping off moving trains, they were quite sure they could do it.

The landings were a little awkward, but effective. The pre-jump lessons they received from the two rail riders whose names they couldn't recall five minutes later, let them hit the ground running. Their first train ride was quite brief, but grandly memorable.

TWENTY-THREE

It would still be the middle of the night when they returned to their own time, so they wouldn't be faced with the problem of escaping the forbidden premises. Their flashlights, still stashed in the bottom of their duffels, should work again once they passed through the green light for the last time, to bring them back into 1965, but the candles were retained just in case. Their Schwinns were well-hidden and waiting, ready to transport them out to the lake, where they would sleep for the remainder of darkness, and then ride back into town for the usual Saturday morning malted milk at the drug store, as if nothing out of the ordinary had occurred.

All went as planned. Jasper Lake was the peaceful retreat it had always been to Shawn and Steve, and this place, this night, seemed more comforting and secure than it ever had, even before the incredible pilgrimage they had just endured, and survived. As they spread out Black Wolf's soft, supple blanket on the beach, their only hope was that they would not discover this had all been a wild dream when they awoke the next morning.

Westland was just as they had left it on the outset, and now it was time to pick up where they left off. The first stop had to be Otis Ramsey's soda fountain. They were long overdue treating their taste buds to one of his thick, creamy delights.

"Good morning, Otis," Shawn beamed with the anticipation of chunks of strawberries blended into Otis' cold, refreshing concoction.

"Mornin,' boys," Otis replied. "Where were you on Saturday? I missed you."

"But this is—"

Steve cut Shawn's statement short with a discrete poke in

the ribs. Apparently, this wasn't Saturday, and until it was determined what day it really was, they'd better come up with some sort of deterrent to squelch the curiosity regarding their absence.

"We've been out camping, and I guess we must have lost track of the days," Steve said calmly. "I'll have chocolate, today."

"And I'll have strawberry, please," Shawn added.

Otis went to work at his usual, methodical pace, preparing the malteds, offering some friendly advice at the same time.

"You guys better let your folks know you're okay. They've been a little worried. They knew you were out camping, but they didn't know where. Yesterday, Mr. Kelly came in asking if I had seen you. He was ready to send out a posse looking for you."

Shawn chuckled. "I think there was a posse looking for us..."

Steve poked him in the ribs again.

Shawn quickly got the message. He dug into his pocket for some change to pay for his malt. Otis immediately recognized the two quarters as currency not of the present era, and he was even more curious when he saw Steve's remittance of similar vintage.

"Where did you get these? Are you sure you want to spend these old coins on ice cream?"

Steve was quick with a reply. "Um... we found them out in the woods where we were camping. It's all we got with us right now. Maybe you can hold them 'till we can bring in some other money."

Otis readily agreed to the terms. He wasn't going to pilfer from his two most loyal customers.

TWENTY-FOUR

Expecting a devastating reprimand now that it was Wednesday, Shawn meekly approached his father at the lumber yard, and in the most apologetic tone he could muster, he reused the excuse Steve had created at the soda fountain. "I guess we just lost track of the time."

Don Kelly was more relieved than he was angry. "Well, next time, at least let us know where you're going. We were worried. Now go let your mother know you're home."

Shawn and Steve were relieved, too. It hadn't been a dream. It was all as real to them as Westland was at that very moment. They now had all the ammunition to tell the actual saga, but who would ever believe it? Chances were pretty good that everyone would hear their story just as another version of an already established legend. Seventy-five years after the fact, there would be little concern by anyone for the two women who died at the hands of the Hawthornes. Nor, would there be any concern that the Hawthorne sisters had so cleverly eluded punishment for their crimes.

Late one afternoon, after nearly a week of making excuses to their friends for why they missed the softball game, and the big party out at the lake, Shawn and Steve sought the seclusion of the rocks on the west edge of town that still remained as one of their escapes from everyday frustrations. There, they could reflect on all they had learned without interruption, and recreate the entire account while it was still fresh in their minds.

Before they ascended to their favorite ledge, Steve circled around to the back side of the huge boulders, and quickly summoned Shawn to observe his discovery. There, nearly lost among the hundreds of etched and painted initials, names, dates, hearts and arrows that had accumulated over the years, was the weathered and worn "X" that Steve had chiseled into the stone, along with the four sets of initials, that recorded for all time the pact of secrecy they had made with Spencer Garett and Brady Pendleton.

If there was no other means to affirm the reality of their experience, to themselves, at least, this certainly indicated that Shawn and Steve had really been there in 1890. Steve dismissed the possibility of using it as proof. No one was going to believe this either.

They perched on their ledge, and recalled every incident in detail from the ride on the lumber wagon to their first meal at the Hotel; from the mysterious, fatal birthday party to the escape from Marshall Flagg's posse; from the brush with Capone to the visit to Dino's Cafe.

They reminded themselves of the remarkable friendships, brief as they were, to be everlasting, unforgettable impressions. They owed their lives to Spencer, Brady, and Jesse.

And who would ever believe a tale describing a scrape with Al Capone, or that the Indian blanket was actually obtained directly from the hands of Black Wolf?

They reminisced the phenomenal changes that occurred over the decades, and the incredible sights that, perhaps few people alive now, had ever witnessed. The church in its glorious frontier grandeur. The forest that nearly covered all of what is now the southern reaches of Westland. The log cabins and farms that eventually gave way to the High School, modern homes, a football field, and a baseball diamond.

A blacksmith shop, and a general store; the old, abandoned barn that protected them from a thunderstorm, and the steam locomotive; horses and buggies, and pickle barrels.

While sorting out the spectrum of details, Shawn and Steve realized they had not only seen historical Westland the way it really was. They had discovered, and solved a crime no one knew happened. They couldn't return to that era to report it. By now their likenesses were probably gracing the walls in Marshall

Flagg's rogue gallery. As victims of circumstance, they were wanted criminals for the disappearance of Wilma Kerns and Alice Page in that time.

Not only had they solved the mystery of the three girls who vanished in 1929, they now knew why the Hawthorne house was never repainted, and why only the windows and doors on the back side of the house were boarded up.

With all the information they had gathered, Shawn and Steve were confident, now, that the Hawthorne ghost sightings in past years were the prostitutes. "Had to be them. They're the only ones who knew about the tunnel."

A thundering gang of ten-year-old cowboys being chased by a relentless tribe of screaming nine-year-old Indians were infiltrating the rocks. Perhaps it was time to relinquish daytime hours here to a new generation of cow pokes and savages. Somehow, even though they were losing their stronghold in this, their domain of solitude, Shawn and Steve graciously accepted the invasion. It was good to know the tradition lived on, and there was always the park gazebo, where the analysis could continue.

The solar rays were casting longer shadows now, but the old house had lost its element of luster, and its ability to capture a sunset in an array of radiant elegance, as Shawn and Steve had witnessed at this time of day, once so long ago. Now, it was nothing more than a drab, weather-beaten old wreck that was still living up to the legend. As Shawn and Steve sat there in the rose garden shelter, they took particular notice of several pedestrians across the street. Twenty feet before they reached the corner of the weed-filled lot, they abruptly changed course, crossed the street, and continued on past the park. When they were well beyond the parameters of their superstitious fear, they crossed back over the street, and resumed their original direction. Another Westland tradition lived on.

It was just about suppertime—time to enjoy a home-cooked

meal in the company of family. Steve and his father were invited to join the Kellys that night for pork chops, mashed potatoes and gravy, and fresh corn-on-the-cob, right out of the Kellys' garden. That combination was one of Steve's favorites, and Kathy Kelly knew how to cook pork chops fit for a king.

Just as they were stepping off the gazebo, something caught Steve's eye.

"Shawn! I saw someone in the upstairs window. I'm not kidding!"

"What window?" Shawn asked, somewhat in disbelief. He thought Steve was just joking with him.

"The one where the pool table is."

"Could you tell who it was? Was it those girls?"

"I don't know, but who else could it be?" Steve was much too serious for this to be a prank. He had seen someone, or something, and Shawn accepted his sincerity.

At last, they had the opportunity to accomplish what they had set out to do so long ago, and they weren't going to sit through a thunderstorm to do it. Never before, in all of their attempts, had they ever caught as much as a glimpse of the slightest movement in any of those windows. Now they were not only going to see the ghosts. They were going to confront them. They knew who the visitors were, and there was absolutely nothing to fear.

They couldn't chance taking the long route to the railroad track. That might take too much time. They darted across the street and into the shadows of the back yard, around the corner of the house and to the cellar entrance, risking the chance of being seen in nearly broad daylight. But this far too important to be concerned with that now.

They had been in and out of that cellar enough times to know exactly where they were going, even without a flashlight. They felt their way along the stone wall, right to the ladder steps. The trap door above was already open, and they were sure they had not left it that way. Not hesitating a second, they negotiated the steps up into the pantry. Through the kitchen and the library, into the parlor, and as if they were in their own house, they dodged past all the furniture and stood at the bottom of the stairway. This was it. The visitors had no other way out.

Suddenly, they heard the crack of the cue ball against the rack, and the clicking of several balls striking one another. Capone's table was getting use, after all these years of sitting idle. They cautiously ascended the darkened stairwell, desperately trying to gain sight of the players, but the filtered sunlight through the dirty windows did not reveal anything to them, until they nearly reached the top.

"You guys play Snooker? Been waiting for you. I was hoping you'd see me in the window and come on up."

Of all the adventures Shawn and Steve had experienced during the past couple of weeks, this had to be the most incredible discovery yet. They stood at the top of the stairs, so astonished they could hardly speak. This was not who they were expecting to see, and the one person farthest from their imagination to be the mystery guest. Could this possibly be the ghost who had mystified so many over the years? Was this the figure on whom the legend mongers had based their ghostly tales?

With cue stick in hand, and a Texas-sized smile, unquestionably happy to see Shawn and Steve, he ruffled his uncombed, short, blonde hair. "I didn't think I'd ever find you again... but I guess I finally did it. What year is this, anyway?"

"Nineteen sixty-five," Steve said, realizing now that Jesse was really there. Expecting two females they had never met, and with whom they would have little in common, instead, Jesse was a welcomed and pleasant surprise.

"How did you get here?" Shawn asked, overlooking the obvious. He was still in a state of total amazement.

"Same way you did. Through the tunnel."

"But how did you find out about it?"

"I've known about the tunnel for a long time, ever since Al

163

was coming around, when Lizz and Emma were in his good graces. I discovered it once when I stashed a bunch of liquor in the cellar, but I never told the Hawthornes or anyone else that I knew about it. I thought Lizz and Emma and the girls they stole from Capone were the only ones who knew about it, until you two showed up in 1930."

"But how did you know we came through it?"

"I had seen you once before, on one of my trips to 1890. Thought you seemed a little misplaced. And then when you were sitting there in the park in '30, looking kind of lost, and just staring at the house, I knew right away how you had gotten there."

"So... what brings you to 1965?"

"I tried quite a few times, and I always wound up in the '50s, '57 mostly. That was pretty scary. I wandered around town a little then. Couldn't believe a newspaper cost thirty-five cents! I'd come back here and stay in the attic for a while, read the paper, and watch everything going on from the windows up there—nighttime mostly, so no one would see me. Sometimes the weather was so stormy I didn't want to go out anyway."

That explained the newspapers on the third floor. That explained the ghosts appearing during thunderstorms. And speculation created another conclusion: Shawn and Steve had widened the time spectrum by opening the portal into later years. They made it possible for Jesse to venture farther than 1957.

Steve looked at Shawn. "Then it wasn't the dam that caused the sightings to stop in '57."

"What sightings? What dam?" Jesse asked.

Steve explained the geographic change Jesse knew nothing about. "You know the valley at the other end of the tunnel? Well, in 1957 a flood control dam was built there. The tunnel entrance was covered, and that whole valley is a big lake now. At first we thought that was the reason no one had come through it since then."

Shawn continued with the explanation. "You see, up until '57, there were a few people who did see you in the windows during the storms. Everyone believed the ghosts of Emma and Lizzy Hawthorne were still in this house. There isn't a single person in this town who will even come near it... except us. And now they want to tear it down, and my dad wants to buy the land to expand his lumber yard."

"Your Dad! Don't the Kellys still own the lumber yard?"

"Don Kelly is my father."

Jesse displayed an expression of surprise, and Shawn realized he might have told more than he should have. But Jesse was a mature being, and he didn't express any hard feelings toward Shawn.

"I know your Dad very well. We practically grew up together, and I guess that makes your grandfather the man who took care of me when my Pop died. Mr. Kelly made sure I had everything I needed 'till I was old enough to start working. He even got me the job at the railroad depot." Steve sensed Shawn's uneasiness with the conversation. It was time to change the subject. "Did you know the Hawthornes killed those two ladies who were found in the house that day we were there?"

"I didn't know for sure, but I always suspected that's what happened."

"So what happened to Emma and Lizzy after we left?"

"They stayed at the Hotel for a week. Left every window in the house open to air it out. Then they left on the train again. That was almost a week ago."

"Did you ever get your Model A?"

"Sure did! Just a couple days ago. And now I'm getting ready to leave town, but I wanted to try one last time to find you."

Shawn shuddered to think Jesse would return to one of the grimmest periods of American history. "Why don't you stay here with us? Life is much better in 1965 than it was—or is—in 1930. And I'd bet my Dad would be really glad to see you again."

"Shawn, your father is fifty-some years old now, and I'm still just twenty. I don't think that would be a very good idea. Besides, your world looks way too complicated. I belong back there... where I'm supposed to be. I'll come back to visit your Dad when the time is right."

They were late for supper, but seeing Jesse again, and finding the last piece of the puzzle was well worth the mild scolding.

TWENTY-FIVE

Don Kelly was settled on the living room couch with every intention of catching up on the current events of the day, the newspaper spread out on his lap, and one ear tuned to the television ten o'clock news in front of him. Shawn didn't usually bother him during his nightly reading and listening routine, but tonight, the younger Kelly had some guilt feelings he had to unload, and lately, his father's busy season schedule left very little time to chat. They had always enjoyed and cherished a strong father/son bond, and even at the age of seventeen, Shawn still found it appropriate to sit shoulder-to-shoulder with his father on the couch, even if there was another four feet of empty couch available. And although he never mentioned it, Don wouldn't have wanted it any other way. He was proud of his offspring's academic accomplishments, but more than that, he was proud of the genuine person Shawn had become, and it was gratifying to know the family business would be passed on to capable and caring hands.

"Dad... I'm really sorry I've been a pain in the ass lately."

Don raised his eyebrows, but his eyes kept focused on the sports page. "What do you mean by that?"

"Well, last week when me and Steve went camping and we stayed out there longer than we should've... and tonight we got back late for supper... we didn't mean to do all that on purpose.

It just happened."

"No harm done." Don turned the page to bury his real emotion in the financial section.

Shawn sensed the necessity for further explanation. "It's just that... well... this is our last summer before we graduate, and next year at this time I'll be going off to college somewhere and I suppose I'll be working most of the time next summer. This is our last chance to be just kids. You know what I mean?"

Mr. Kelly glanced away from the paper. He was impressed with Shawn's mature observation of accepting an implied responsible role in his not-so-distant adult future. That statement re-assured him that Shawn was headed for success, and as a little advance reward, he would recognize and respect Shawn's concern of wanting to be a kid for the rest of the summer.

"Yes, Shawn, I know exactly what you mean. I only wish I would've had that attitude when I was your age."

Shawn saw his opportunity to squeeze out a bit of information he had never heard his dad talk about.

"Me and Steve are probably just like you and Jesse were back then."

Don put down the paper, and a touch of astonishment took up residency on his face.

"Jesse! How do you know about Jesse?"

"Um... I guess I heard you mention him once or twice... and I just happened to think of it now."

Don rubbed his chin, and thoughts of his own youthful years sparkled in his eyes.

"Jesse was a good friend. He lost his parents when he was very young. We took him in for a while, and your Grandpa Kelly treated him like one of his own. Those were hard times, but Jesse always managed to land on his feet... saved all his money, and one day he pulled up in front of the lumber yard in a brand new Model A Ford... had to show it to Grandpa Kelly before anyone else. He was so proud of that car. Not too long after that, he left town, and I don't know where he ever ended up. Never saw him after that."

Now Shawn knew he shouldn't expect to see Jesse playing Snooker in the Hawthorne house again. Today must've been his last trip through the tunnel. But another thought occurred to Shawn, one that might brighten his father's spirit.

"You never know! Maybe he'll show up again someday... and he'll probably be driving a Lincoln."

TWENTY-SIX

With less than a month until school began for another year, there hardly seemed time for all the usual summertime activities, much less, a visit to a nursing home. But Steve insisted that Shawn come with him. He had been there with his father the day before visiting a distant relative he hardly knew, and noticed something there that Shawn had to see for himself.

Westland Nursing Home was one of the most recent, modern additions to the city's outskirts. From outward appearances it looked more like an apartment building, but inside the main entrance, there was no mistaking this facility for nothing short of a hospital.

Shawn was completely in the dark. He had no idea why Steve had drug him into this place overflowing with people he did not recognize, and Steve wasn't giving him the slightest clue. But he trusted Steve's judgment, and when they reached the nurses' station at the east wing, and Steve asked the attendant there "Is it okay if we visit the gentleman in room one twenty-four?" Shawn was confident Steve knew what he was doing.

"Sure. I'll bet he'd love to have some company today," the nurse said with a smile, and pointed them down the corridor.

"Thank you, Ma'am. I know where it is."

They approached the open door, and Steve pointed to the name plaque on the wall next to it. Suddenly, the fog lifted from this secretive mission, as Shawn read the name.

His hair was white, and his face held a pale, withdrawn expression. His body was frail and weak, and the movements were slow and deliberate, as he made his way from the window to the plush, high-backed arm chair, carefully lowering himself into it. Brady Pendleton was 89, and he had returned to Westland to live out his final years.

The burden of explaining who they were, and why they were there, would be the most difficult task Shawn and Steve had faced. Without any preparation, they weren't even sure where to begin.

"Hello, Mr. Pendleton."

"Hello, Brady."

The old man remained comfortably seated in his chair with a custom hand-carved, highly polished wooden cane resting against the chair front between his knees.

"Hello, boys," he replied, seemingly delighted to have visitors.

Before Steve could begin speaking again, Mr. Pendleton was reaching for a pair of eye glasses on the small nightstand beside him. He put on the spectacles, and obviously studying the two lads standing before him he asked, "Don't I know you two from somewhere?"

"Yes, Brady... you do. I'm Steve."

"And I'm Shawn."

Steve began to realize this might not be so difficult, after all.

"You and Spencer... a campfire in the woods across the road from the Hawthorne house. You'd been fishing at Miller's Pond. The next day we split firewood out behind the Blacksmith Shop, and then we all went swimming at Raccoon Holler. And then we all came back and ate supper at Spencer's house."

Brady Pendleton just sat calmly, listening intently to every word.

Shawn continued with the seventy-five-year-old itinerary. "The next day, we saw Black Wolf on the street, and I bought the blanket from him. And that night we saw the Hawthorne twins poison those two other women and haul the bodies away in a buggy behind a white horse..."

Steve intervened. "Cleo. The horse's name was Cleo. He came from P.T. Barnum's Circus."

Brady's face was beaming with joyous amazement as Shawn went on.

"Then we all took an oath of secrecy, and Steve and I had to hide in Garett's hay loft and you and Spencer rode us out to the valley and led the posse that was chasing us up the valley so we could get away."

Brady didn't know how these two boys, in 1965, could possibly have all this information. They certainly appeared as the two drifters he remembered, and the events they were describing were quite vivid memories he had carried with him throughout his lifetime. But there was one detail they couldn't possibly know. It would be the final test of their validity.

"But before you left that night..." Brady paused, to carefully choose the right words. "You gave me something. Do you remember?"

Shawn smiled. He knew he was being tested. "I gave you a five-dollar gold piece, for good luck."

"And I gave one to Spencer, too," Steve added.

Brady pulled open a drawer in the nightstand, and when his hand emerged, it was holding the two Half Eagles, brightly polished, and each strung on gold neck chains. He held them out for Shawn and Steve to examine.

"I don't know how it's possible. No one could have known that. We never told anyone."

"Why do you have both pieces?" Steve asked. "Where is Spencer?"

The old man's face turned a little sad. "Spencer gave me his just before he died about three years ago. "We always figured they really were lucky. As long as we had these things hanging around our necks, good things happened. Then one day, Spencer left his in his room... out in Portland we were, working on the riverboats on the Columbia. The dang fool slipped and fell on a loading dock and broke his dad burn leg."

"So what have you been doing all these years?" Shawn asked.

"Just after World War One, we bought our own boat. Northern Lights we called her. Ferried cars and passengers across the bay at Astoria every day for thirty-three years. Never will forget the day we made our last trip and retired... November third, 1951."

The entire afternoon just slipped away as Shawn and Steve, like children hearing bedtime stories, listened to Brady's tales of the true wild, wild West. His ability to deliver them was just as entertaining now, as it had been the first night they met. Only now, his English had improved.

As they were preparing to leave, with the promise to visit again soon, Brady requested his long lost friends to come close to his side, and as they honored his petition, he draped the golden chains around their necks. "Hang on to these... for good luck... I want you to have them now, and I know Spencer would, too."

Only Shawn and Steve would ever really know the true meaning of these tokens. Although the actual value was great, to them, the gold coins were priceless in terms only they could understand.

Steve pulled out his pocket watch just as a nurse came into the room to check on Mr. Pendleton.

"Wow! Where did you get that neat watch?" she asked as she admired the handsome timepiece.

Steve just smiled. "The Emporium... at the other end of the tunnel."

MISSISSIPPI PIRATES

MISSISSIPPI PIRATES
J.L. Fredrick

1.

Peter stumbled from the bed to the washstand, fumbled in the dim lantern light for a firm-enough grip on the pitcher handle, and gently poured an ample amount of room temperature water into the basin. His eyes felt like a dry creek bed from a much too brief sleep. He'd come awake slowly with the hammering of a fist on the door and a gravelly voice alerting him that the train would leave in an hour. By that he knew it must be six a.m. as the train was scheduled to leave at seven, and now he mildly anticipated the side pork and cornbread breakfast in the hotel dining room.

He thought back about the many times he had made this trip before the Southern Minnesota Railroad made life easier. His father owned a little country general store, and at first he had accompanied him on this trip to La Crosse a few times to learn the inventory purchasing procedure. Then, later on, when he grew a little older and became known by the warehouse operators where he did business, Peter started making the trip alone, allowing his father to keep the store open.

In those days, the trip involved a long stagecoach ride to Rushford one day, and then the next day he would sit in the crisp pre-dawn air on the wooden bench outside the Rushford Hotel waiting for the Burbank Stage Lines coach to arrive from the livery. In just a short while, he and several other passengers would be rocking and jostling their way on another all-day ride in the Concord stagecoach to La Crescent, where on the following morning a ferryboat took him across the Mississippi River to La Crosse. Sometimes, a mid-trip breakdown or a mud hole would delay the stagecoach trip into another day. But if the timing was right, he could conduct his business at the various warehouses the next day, and have the store goods loaded on a barge that would be taken up the Root River to Rushford by a little steamboat early the next morning.

Now, though, instead of waiting for a stagecoach at Rushford, he waited for the train outside the *Phoenix Hotel* in Lanesboro, the finest and most comfortable traveling accommodations in Southern Minnesota. The *Phoenix* had been one of the first business concerns of the Townsite Company when Lanesboro was in its infant years. Completed in 1870 as the result of need for a hotel—because the railroad had inspired the birth of the new town as an ideal location for a terminal—the *Phoenix* housed business offices, the Bank, a saloon, and its lower level served as ticket office and baggage room for the railroad. Peter enjoyed this part of the journey; he always came the day before, withdrew traveling and purchasing money from his bank account, devoured a delicious supper, and then indulged in a few cold beers at the saloon with friends, all without leaving the hotel. That's why his night had seemed so short, because this time he had stayed at the pub much too long before retiring to his room. He should have been well-rested, fresh and alert for the day's travel, but alas, he felt physically drained.

2.

In the early morning light Peter examined the list he pulled from the inside breast pocket of his coat as he sat on the boarding platform bench waiting for the train to arrive from Fountain. He had recently been placed in charge of the inventory and the store's operation so that his father could focus more time on launching another new, lucrative business—a lumber yard and hardware store. Peter welcomed the responsibility, but sometimes he experienced sudden pangs of uncertainty, concerned with his ability to properly prepare an adequate list of goods to be picked up. But his father trusted him, and he knew that he had to do this on his own now, as the store would soon be his sole responsibility. At eighteen years of age, he had been given the opportunity to build his future from the foundation that his father had built from almost nothing. He had to prove himself worthy.

Peter glanced around the platform where a number of people had gathered—other travelers, some going to the next town, and some going to far-away places. He dared not pull out the money folded in his pocket to make sure of its presence, as too many people could observe him; three hundred dollars could be much too encouraging for some dishonest soul to wait for the right, unsuspecting moment to relieve him of it. But he patted his coat breast discretely to make certain it was there.

He heard the chugging locomotive in the passes cut through the hills to the west and then the shrill whistle interrupted everything that might have been going on in the town. The train slowly rumbled across the trestle spanning the Root River just above the mill pond. In just a few minutes he would be able to settle into a comfortable seat aboard the passenger car, and with a little luck he wouldn't have some busybody sitting next to him asking him where he was going, the nature of his trip, and how long he would stay. Not that Peter was unsociable. But today he'd rather sit back, close his eyes, and try to make up for the short night. Yes, the train was making this journey much more agreeable than stagecoaches had ever allowed, not to mention less time consuming; the trip to La Crescent would only take a couple of hours, as opposed to the two-day journey aboard a stage. But a couple of hours would be enough time to rejuvenate his tired body.

"Good morning, Peter," the conductor said in his vibrant welcoming tone. "On your way to La Crosse, I see," he added as he eyed the ticket Peter handed over.

"Good morning, Sam," the young man replied.

"Back to the warehouses again so soon?"

"We've been really busy this summer," Peter said. "It'll be a bigger shipment than usual, too, this time."

"Coming over by boat in a couple of days?" the conductor asked. He had become familiar with Peter's operation simply by repetition, and Peter stuck to a regular schedule on these trips.

"Yes, Sam, same as usual."

"Well, make yourself comfortable," Sam said. "You look a little tired today." Then the conductor moved on to greet the next passengers.

The next stop at the little village of Whalan was brief, as usual, only long enough to board a half-dozen passengers and exchange mail bags. It seemed to be a light traveling day, as only a fraction of the available coach space was occupied; Peter felt fortunate to enjoy an entire seat to himself, so sprawling a little allowed him to get comfortable. He slept right through the rest of the stops at Peterson, Rushford, Houston, and Hokah. But when the train arrived at Grand Crossing, just below La Crescent, the conductor shook his shoulder. "Peter," he said. "We're here. Wake up!"

Peter bolted upright from a sounder sleep than he thought possible on a moving train. "Thank you, Sam," he muttered, embarrassed. The train was already stopped, so he rose from his seat, stretched, and stepped out into the aisle. "I'll see you in a couple of days, Sam," he told the conductor, and started making his way to the exit.

Sam smiled and waved. "See you in a couple of days," he repeated. Sam knew Peter's routine almost as well as his own.

It was here that Peter would contact the captain of *Little Frank*, a small steamboat that would transport his purchased goods from the La Crosse harbor to the railhead at Grand Crossing, just as it had done many times in the past. Since the introduction of rail service west to Lanesboro, the little steamboats that had once been the important factor in moving cargo up the Root River valley had ceased the difficult navigation on that shallow, narrow, winding stream. Now, they simply ferried the goods across the Mississippi, as there was still no bridge connecting Wisconsin with Minnesota.

On this pleasant summer day Peter strolled casually to the levee. He breathed in the river air that always seemed different than that of the woodlands where he lived. Always a pleasure to come here, he enjoyed the sights of the Mississippi—the bold, rocky bluffs, the majestic boats, and the alluring, grand old waterway itself. He lingered as long as he dared, taking it all in.

A while later, as Peter shook hands with Captain David Foster of the Little Frank, he heard the shrill whistle of the locomotive, and then he heard the conductor's familiar final call *"All aboard!"* He waved to Sam standing on the steps of the passenger coach as the train slowly pulled away.

"When will your freight be ready to load?" Captain Foster asked.

"I'll have all the goods delivered from the warehouses to the La Crosse harbor by tomorrow afternoon, and it will be more than usual," Peter informed the captain. "You'll be able to load everything tomorrow night. I'll hire Frenchy to guard it until you arrive. The Southern Minnesota is expecting to load it in one of their boxcars early Wednesday morning."

"Rest assured, Peter," the captain said. "We'll take it over sometime after midnight and it'll be on their loading platform before five o'clock."

"Thank you, David," Peter said. "Now, I'd better catch a ferry to La Crosse."

Captain Foster pointed. "Better hurry," he urged Peter. "The *McRoberts* will be shoving off in a few minutes. Otherwise you'll be waiting a couple of hours for the next one."

Peter turned to look. "Thanks, again," he said as he waved and scurried off to the dock.

After the two-hour nap on the train, Peter felt awake and alert; he filled his lungs with the fresh river valley air as the *McRoberts* made its way to the La Crosse landing. He had a busy two days ahead of him, but now he felt ready to meet the challenge.

3.

The largest procurement Peter had ever gathered for his store lay in huge stacks at the La Crosse harbor the next evening waiting for *Little Frank's* crew to stow it aboard the steamer. Barrels of pickles, salt pork, whiskey and crackers; sacks of flour and corn meal, sugar, and coffee beans; crates of canned goods, spices, and vegetables; bolts of gingham and cotton cloth; ready-made shirts and dresses, hats and leather gloves; axes and shovels, rope and kegs of nails; pots and pans and various other household wares. Peter was almost certain that his store would soon need to expand.

He stayed by his goods until a little past six o'clock. He had left word with Mr. Kellogg at the Western Enterprise Hotel to relay a message to Frenchy, the young boy who had been highly recommended by the riverboat crew, the boy he trusted to guard his stacks of merchandise until the ferryboat crew came to take them across the river. Frenchy tended cows, one of which was Mr. Kellogg's, out in a country pasture; he returned the cows to

180

their barns about six o'clock, collected his pay from Mr. Kellogg, and then he would come to relieve Peter.

When Frenchy arrived, Peter went to the hotel for his evening meal, and then, as always, brought Frenchy a generous basket of food for his supper, and paid him two dollars for his night's guard duty.

Peter retired in his room at the Western Enterprise that night contented with the past two day's business. He was pleased with his purchases, including the various new gadgets that his patrons would surely be glad to see. The next morning he could enjoy a leisurely breakfast, and then catch a ferryboat across the river to meet the train at Grand Crossing. So far, this trip had been not much different from any other.

4.

Frenchy was happy to see Captain Foster and his crew tie up the Little Frank at the levee just after midnight. "*Bonsoir, M'sieur* Foster," he called out as the captain sauntered along the levee with a lantern searching for his cargo.

"Ah, there you are, Frenchy," the captain greeted the boy. "Peter said you'd be here as usual."

"*Oui, mon ami.* These are his goods."

"So, how are you, Frenchy?"

"*J'ai besoin de dormir*... I am so very tired. I tended the cattle all day, too."

"Any trouble here tonight?" Foster asked.

"Oh, no, Captain. Some men came by after dark, spying all the goods here, but when they saw me, they ran back to their *bateau* and paddled away."

"Pilfers," said Captain Foster. "Well, I s'pect we won't see them anymore tonight. You did a good job, Frenchy."

"*Merci*, Captain."

Captain Foster couldn't help but notice that Frenchy barely kept his eyes open. "Frenchy... would you like to sleep in my cabin on the Little Frank? You look too tired to paddle your canoe over to the Island." He was truly concerned about the boy's safety; crossing the river to his father's cabin on Barron's Island in the dark could be treacherous for someone so tired.

"That is very kind of you, M'sieur, but I couldn't be of such bother—"

"Nonsense... it's no bother," insisted the captain. "My First Mate will show you the way, and we'll load your canoe onboard so it will be right there when you want it."

The boy was practically sleeping where he stood. "*Merci,*" he managed to respond. The First Mate guided him to the captain's cabin up on the Texas deck and put him to bed.

Fourteen-year-old Frenchy was well-known on the La Crosse waterfront, and beloved by all the riverboat crews. His Winnebago Indian mother was dead, and his father, a left-over from the French-Canadian fur traders, often abandoned the boy for long interludes to fend for himself. But Frenchy was quite capable of seeing to his own needs. His Indian uncles and cousins had taught him hunting and survival skills, swimming, and the all-important art of maneuvering a canoe on the river. He rarely asked for help, but modestly accepted when it was offered.

Frenchy slept quite soundly for a couple of hours while the Little Frank's crew loaded the crates and barrels of Peter Story's merchandise. He only woke momentarily when the whistle atop the pilothouse sounded, announcing the steamer's departure from the levee, but he soon fell asleep again.

5.

As the little freighter steamed away from the La Crosse harbor making its way southward around Barron's Island, another boat lay moored in a slough on the lower end of the island, hidden from sight from any part of the city. At the southern tip of the island, two members of its crew listened for Little Frank's whistle and watched for its lights as it left the harbor. They had plenty of time to return to their craft.

When Captain Foster navigated Little Frank around the isle and headed southwest toward Grand Crossing on the Minnesota side of the river, he did not notice the black shrouded corsair with no lights slither silently out of its hiding place. So well was its appearance masked in the moonless dark night, none of the crew aboard Little Frank saw it until it was beside them and ropes were lashing the two boats together. Unarmed, Little Frank's deckhands were helpless against the pirate's guns, and although no shots were fired, the engineer and crewmen, their attempted resistance futile, were swiftly bludgeoned by the invaders rushing over the gunwales.

In the pilothouse, Captain Foster couldn't see what was happening on the deck below, but he suspected the inevitable. He tried to steer his vessel away, but to no avail. It was too late, and everything was happening too quickly to avoid falling prey to pirates. Out in the middle of the river on a dark night, there was little hope that any other boats would see or hear; little hope that anyone would know to come to their aid.

It seemed to Foster that only seconds had passed since Little Frank had been violated by the pirates when the engines were silenced. His signals to the engineer for more steam had rendered no response and his control was nonexistent. An instant later, the pilothouse door crashed open. Another instant and Captain Foster lay on the pilothouse floor, his head bleeding from a severe blow by the butt of a rifle.

With the crew incapacitated, the privateers went to work transferring the entire cargo from the Little Frank's deck to their black boat, so well-disguised that it was nearly invisible. When they were finished, they cut the Little Frank loose to drift on the current and disappeared into the night.

All the commotion during the fracas awoke Frenchy. He knew the noises he heard weren't normal. He rose out of the bunk and peered out the window to see the sinister looking vessel alongside the Little Frank. Curious of the events taking place, his silent Indian footsteps led him to the ladder up to the pilothouse. There he found Captain Foster on the floor.

"Mon Dieu!" he cried softly and put his ear to the Captain's chest. Foster's heart was still beating, but there seemed little that Frenchy could do to help him. Stealthily he climbed down the ladder to the gangway above the cargo deck. From there, keeping himself concealed from their view, he watched as the pirates moved the crates of Peter's merchandise onto the deck of the black boat and extinguish all of Little Frank's lights. As they loosed the ropes lashing the two boats together and pushed off, Frenchy slipped down to the cargo deck. "Mon Dieu!" he cried out again upon stumbling over the bodies of the deckhands.

Then he remembered that Captain Foster had told him his canoe would be onboard. He took a match from his pocket, struck it on the deck and used its light to locate a lantern hanging within easy reach. Lantern lit, he set out to find his canoe. It was at the bow. He could still hear the chuffing steam of the pirate boat. He knew he couldn't help any of this crew now; the Little Frank was adrift and would surely run aground somewhere downriver, and there was nothing he could do about that, either. But there was something he could do—he could try to follow the pirate boat. The pirates would have to hide before dawn. When he found out where they hid, he could go for help.

He slid his canoe off the bow deck and within seconds he was trailing after the sound of the invisible steamer. An hour later, he knew he was well below Two Mile Island at Brownsville. His arms ached as he tried to keep pace with the steamer—at least stay within earshot. First light of day was near, and the sound of the steamer was heading toward the Wisconsin shore, where Frenchy was certain it would slip into a slough, out of sight from the main channel. Then the engine's sound trail stopped. The final exhaust of steam swished away into the stillness of the early morning.

Frenchy had fished these waters and hunted these riverbanks countless times, and he knew there were many sloughs here where a shallow-draft boat could easily be hidden in the back waters. It was the perfect place for pirates to hide by day, and to emerge without being seen to strike by night.

The gray outline of trees on the bank started to appear. Frenchy paddled his canoe as silently as possible, hugging closely to the reeds along the shoreline, and then turned into the mouth of a slough. Just beyond, the backwaters opened up in several directions; he took the channel to the right, as it seemed deeper than the rest, and there was a slight current, so he knew there was an outlet farther downstream, the ideal place for a boat to hide behind the wooded island formed by the channel.

The channel curved back, away from the river. Frenchy thought he heard voices. He stopped paddling and listened. As his canoe slid silently, slowly along, the voices became more distinct, and then, through the trees around the next bend to the right, he could just barely make out the shape of a small riverboat. He grounded the canoe and sneaked through the trees to get a better look. Several men were at work pulling big black canvas tarpaulins onto the upper deck, canvas that had been draped over the superstructure to conceal the customary riverboat white during hours of darkness. When the tarpaulins were all rolled up and stowed out of sight behind a railing, the men began unloading their booty onto a flat bottom barge that was tied up to trees at water's edge. By then, the morning was bright enough for Frenchy to recognize the crates he had been guarding the night before, and he was quite certain these were the same men who had come prowling the La Crosse levee.

But this was no place for him to be now; he had no weapons with which to protect himself against these brutal scoundrels who had injured—perhaps killed—the crew of the Little Frank. His bow and arrows lay bundled in the canoe, but he knew that alone he would be no match against this many men with guns. The best option was to retreat back to the river and get to Brownsville on the other side, the nearest place where he might find help.

6.

By the time he reached Brownsville, the broad bright of day had unfolded. He had seen nothing of the Little Frank or its crew; it had to still be somewhere upriver from the village. A few of the townsmen had gathered at the General Store drinking their morning coffee and smoking their pipes. Nearly exhausted, using the last bit of energy he had left, he darted into the store. *"Sacre Bleu!"* he cried out. "The Little Frank has been attacked by pirates!"

Somewhat startled by the dark-skinned boy's hysterical outbreak, the men stared at him for a long moment.

"Somebody must help them! The crew... they are all badly hurt!" the boy pleaded.

"How do you know all this?" one of the men asked.

"I was on Little Frank... sleeping in a bunk on the upper deck when it happened. The pirates did not know I was there."

"Where is the Little Frank now?"

"I do not know... I followed the pirate bateau in my canoe to a slough downriver. Then I came here. Will you please help Captain Foster and his crew? The Little Frank was adrift and has probably run aground."

"Where did this happen?" the men asked.

"Just below Barron's Island. They were taking cargo to the railhead at Grand Crossing."

"And you say you followed the pirates to a slough? Where?"

"Maybe two or three miles downriver from here."

"How many were on the pirate boat? Did you get a good look at them?"

"Maybe six... maybe more... it was dark."

"Can you take us there?"

"Oui, I can show you... but first, you must find Little Frank and help Captain Foster."

The men huddled together to discuss the validity of the boy's story. "I have heard of this sort of thing happening," one of the men said. "Maybe this French speaking Indian boy is one of them. Maybe this is one of their tricks."

"No," said another. "I've seen this boy before... he's quite well-known at the La Crosse harbor. All the riverboat men seem to like him. I don't think it's a trap."

"Then let's get some skiffs launched. We'll look for the Little Frank, and then we'll have the boy show us the way to the pirates' cove."

"I am too tired to help row," said Frenchy. "But I must come with you to find Little Frank."

"Very well. You can come. What's your name?"

"I am Frenchy... my father is Henri Bouton, the trader on Barron's Island."

"And why were you aboard Little Frank?"

"I was watching their cargo they were to pick up at the La Crosse levee, but I was too tired to get home, and Captain Foster let me sleep in his bunk."

They put Frenchy in the bow of one of the skiffs and eight men set out to find the lost steamer.

7.

When Peter woke, sunlight glistened on the river's surface outside his hotel room window. Well-rested and feeling good, he was anxious to get his breakfast, and then begin his journey home. He would be back in Lanesboro by early afternoon, and barring any railroad delays, he would have his wagonload of goods at his store by sundown.

News of the Little Frank's fate had not yet reached La Crosse when Peter boarded the ferry to Grand Crossing. He saw nothing of Frenchy or of his freight at the levee, so he presumed everything was going according to schedule. At the railhead he located the freight master. "I don't see my goods anywhere on the platform," he said. "So I can assume that you have it loaded in a boxcar?"

"Oh, Mr. Story," the railroad man replied. "Your merchandise never arrived here this morning."

"What do you mean, never arrived? It wasn't at the levee in La Crosse. I checked before I came over."

"Well, it didn't get here."

"Then it must still be on the Little Frank," Peter said. "Have you seen the boat or Captain Foster?"

"Haven't seen 'em."

This wasn't like Captain Foster; he had always been dependable in the past on many occasions. Nor was it like Frenchy; he had always been trustworthy. Had there been any trouble, they would have alerted the hotel clerk. Something had gone terribly wrong—something that had prevented the captain or the boy from coming forth with justification.

Seeing that Peter was quite distraught, the railroad freight clerk made an attempt to settle his uneasiness: "They could've had engine trouble. The Little Frank could've been towed to the

McDonald boatyard for repairs," he said.

"And when I find it there," Peter said, "Can you still g͟e͟ cargo loaded on a later train today?"

"I think that is entirely possible," said the railroad man.

"Good... and would you please instruct Sam, the conductor to somehow get a message to my father... that I will be delayed?"

Peter saw that the ferry had not yet departed for La Crosse. He hurried back to the dock and boarded. When the ferry landed at the La Crosse levee, Peter caught a horse car northbound to the boatyard.

"We haven't seen the Little Frank," said the foreman at the boatyard. "Nor have we had word that she was in trouble and needed a tow."

"The Little Frank picked up my cargo at the levee last night," Peter explained. "Captain Foster assured me that it would be delivered to the railhead at Grand Crossing this morning, but they never arrived there. Do you have any idea where they might have gone?"

"If she developed engine or boiler trouble out in the river, the current could've carried her downstream toward Brownsville, but if she had no power, Cap'n Foster wouldn't have much control of where she went... maybe no steam so he couldn't use the whistle to signal anybody on shore for help, either. Best he could do would be to throw out an anchor."

8.

The Brownsville men found Little Frank helplessly, silently aground on a sandbar at the head of Two Mile Island, just upriver from the village. She didn't appear to be wrecked—just aground. Crewmen sat on the main deck, holding their heads, moaning in pain, some tending to the injuries of others. The engineer paced about in a daze, a nasty wound on the side of his head. Frenchy scrambled aboard and immediately started for the hurricane deck and the pilothouse with another of the rescuers on his heels. They helped Captain Foster to his feet, but he could not stand on his own, so they sat him on the lazy man's bench at the rear of the pilothouse.

"What happened?" he mumbled. He seemed to recognize Frenchy, but the recent events were nothing but a blur.

"Little Frank was attacked by pirates," Frenchy informed him. "They stole your cargo and left you adrift."

"Where are we?" the captain moaned.

"On a sandbar at Two Mile Island."

"The crew? Are they—"

"They are injured, like you, but they are okay," Frenchy said reassuringly. "Some other men are tending to them right now."

The man who followed Frenchy to the pilothouse said, "I'm gonna find something for that cut on his head," and then he left.

"The boat," said Captain Foster. "Is the boat damaged?"

"She looks okay," Frenchy replied. "Just run aground on this sandbar."

"The cargo," Foster said. "We were taking cargo to Grand Crossing." Gradually, the captain's senses were restoring as he sorted out his thoughts. Not everything was entirely clear to him, but he was beginning to reconnoiter the memories of what had occurred a few hours earlier and the sight of Frenchy and the sound of his voice was helping Foster now to remember.

"The cargo is gone, Captain, but I know where it is," the boy told him.

The captain looked at Frenchy, puzzled.

"I followed the pirate bateau," Frenchy said."

Captain Foster still seemed in a quandary.

"Don't you remember, Captain? You loaded my canoe on Little Frank, and I slept in your cabin while your crew loaded Peter's cargo."

The Brownsville man returned with a cool, wet towel and began swabbing Foster's head wound.

"Yes," the captain said. "Now I remember... you were guarding Peter's merchandise, and the First Mate put you to bed in my quarters. Peter's cargo... we must try to find Peter's goods."

"Don't worry," Frenchy said, laying his hand on Foster's forearm. "I know where it is."

"Oh, yes, you said that. Then we should go after it." The captain tried to stand, but with great difficulty. "What is your name?" he asked the man tending his wound.

"Jim... Jim Bennett," he replied.

Jim pressured Captain Foster back to his seat. "Not so fast, Captain," he said. "You're in no condition to go fighting pirates right now."

"Says who? Are you a doctor?"

"No," Jim replied. "I'm a shop keeper in Brownsville, but I help Doc Riley every now and then, and I know enough to see we need to get you and your crew to him."

"But Peter's goods... we need to get them back."

Just then a steam whistle sounded from out in the channel. Frenchy quickly jerked his head around to see the Belle Rosa, a log rafter returning upriver after delivering a raft of logs to a mill at Clinton. He jumped to his feet, pushed the window open and leaned out as far as he could without falling, waving his arms and yelling "CAPTAIN JOHN! CAPTAIN JOHN! STOP! WE NEED YOUR HELP!"

Frenchy heard some of the men on the lower deck calling out to the rafter as well. Within a couple of minutes, the Belle Rosa was as near as it could get without running aground on the sandbar. A couple of her crewmen jumped overboard into chest-deep water, swam, and then waded to Little Frank.

"What happened here?" they asked as they climbed aboard.

"Attacked by pirates," a Little Frank deckhand told them.

"Pirates!" they responded in disbelief. There had been no such occurrences in quite some time.

"Yeah... they knocked us all cold, stole our cargo and set us adrift."

"What did their boat look like? We've met several southbound boats this morning."

"Couldn't tell... it was draped with black canvas to hide it in the dark."

"Scoundrels! Stuck on this sandbar, I see. We can try to pull you off."

"That would be good," said Little Frank's First Mate. "But we don't have steam up, and our engineer isn't in any shape to run the machinery, and our captain certainly can't pilot this boat back to La Crosse."

"Then we'll tow you back to La Crosse. The Belle Rosa is a very powerful craft. She'll take you upriver easy."

"As First Mate of Little Frank, I'll take you up on your offer."

9.

At Brownsville, the entire little river town was outraged knowing that pirates loomed nearby. To assault the crew and steal the cargo of a local trade vessel upon these waters was preposterous; the rogues had to be brought to justice. More men had joined the village marshal forming a posse to pursue the pirates. Heavily armed with hunting rifles and shotguns, they waited for the return of the search party that went to rescue the crew of Little Frank, and the French speaking Indian boy who said he could lead them to where the pirates had taken the loot. The crew of another steamer, the Wenona, was heating up her boiler and preparing for the mission. She was a small but rugged low-draft boat that had been built for the Root River trade, and was capable of navigating the shallow back water sloughs. If the boy was right about the pirate camp, the Wenona could get the posse to them.

As the eight men of the search party rowed their skiffs toward the Brownsville landing with only the boy as an extra passenger, curiosity filled the eyes of the people looking on from the bank.

"Did you find the Little Frank?" someone called out when the boats were still thirty yards out.

"We did," was the answer. "And the Belle Rosa is towing her to La Crosse."

"How's the crew?" Doc Riley called out. He had joined the crowd of people at the landing, quite certain that his services would be needed.

"They're all alive—some badly hurt—but they are alive! They all stayed with the boat and they'll get medical attention at La Crosse."

The four skiffs carrying the eight men and Frenchy nosed up to the landing. Others were there to help them ashore.

"Where's the boy?" Marshal Calkins asked. "Can he guide us, now, to the pirates' camp?"

Frenchy was so exhausted that he had fallen asleep in the bow of the skiff. Even the bright sunlight on his face or the tumult all around him had not aroused him from his sleep.

"Is he dead?" someone cried.

Doc Riley rushed to the rowboat and quickly examined the boy. "He'll be fine," Doc said. "He's just fatigued, and he needs some rest. I can imagine that this has been quite stressful... even for a youngster."

"But the pirates," one of the vigilantes said. "He's the only one who knows where they are."

"The pirates aren't apt to be on the move in broad daylight," said Marshal Calkins. "They'll wait for the cover of darkness. We have plenty of time. Let the boy rest for a while."

10.

Peter remained on the wharf near the McDonald boatyard with hopes that the Little Frank would eventually turn up, or, at least, that he would hear word of its whereabouts. He was quite relieved when he heard that Belle Rosa had towed the stricken steamer to the levee, but shocking was the news of the entire crew, now at a downtown hotel and in the care of Dr. McArthur.

"They were attacked by pirates," Captain John Alexander told Peter.

"Pirates!" exclaimed Peter. "Why, that's ridiculous! Pirates are on the seas, not the Mississippi River!"

"Oh, but they are," said Captain John. "Where there's water and boats carrying cargo, there's pirates. Since the Civil War ended, they've come farther north."

"So... my merchandise that was on Little Frank has been commandeered by pirates?"

"'Fraid so," said Captain John. "But you might be in luck. Frenchy followed them in his canoe, and he said he knows where the pirates are camped."

"Frenchy?"

"All of us here on the riverfront know Frenchy... he's a young boy who spends a lot of time around here—"

"Yes, I know who Frenchy is," Peter interrupted. I hire him to watch my goods on the levee until the boat picks it up."

"Well, lucky for you that he was aboard Little Frank." The captain continued to explain how the boy had courageously followed the pirate vessel downriver through the darkness and discovered their hideout in a backwater slough.

"Where is Frenchy now?" Peter asked.

"He returned to Brownsville with the men who came to Little Frank's aid. He's gonna lead them to the pirates' camp. But we told them to wait until the Sheriff arrived... that we would get word to the lawmen and bring them to Brownsville."

A short while later the County Sheriff and his posse arrived at the wharf, armed and ready to make the trip to Brownsville aboard Belle Rosa.

"Sheriff," Peter said. "I want to accompany you on the Belle Rosa to Brownsville."

The sheriff eyed the young man up and down. "I've got six men already, and if I know Calkins, he'll have a whole army organized down there by now. I don't need any more."

"But I'm Peter Story... I rightfully own the goods that the pirates stole from Little Frank."

"You're Peter Story?"

"Yes, sir."

"Well... I got that name from Captain Foster, too. I guess it will be okay." Then as an afterthought he added, "You'll stay in Brownsville, though, when we go after them."

"But I'm good with a rifle—"

"You'll stay in Brownsville or you don't go at all," the sheriff said sternly.

11.

It was just past noon when the two posses boarded the Wenona and began planning their strategy. They were twenty in number, ready for action. Still a little groggy after a sound sleep, Frenchy was there too, and his canoe lay on the cargo deck among seven other skiffs. He would guide Wenona's pilot to the mouth of the slough, and then, in his canoe he would lead the other men in their rowboats on a stealth approach to the pirates' camp. Peter remained at the Brownsville landing and watched the Wenona steam away downriver.

Captain John of the Belle Rosa came over to talk as a friendly gesture, seeing Peter standing all alone. "Sheriff wouldn't let you go with the search party?"

"No... and I don't know why," Peter replied. "I'm just as good with a gun as anybody."

"Could get dangerous. If this is the same gang that hit here before... a few years back... they're not shy about killing. Killed a boat captain and a deputy sheriff when they went after them."

"You mean they didn't get captured?"

"Nope. They slipped away never to be seen again... until now."

"Think it's the same ones?"

"Could be... but now that Frenchy has seen how they disguised their boat during the attack, and saw what it looked like without the disguise, they won't get away so easily."

"Poor Frenchy," Peter sighed. "He looked so tired."

"Don't worry 'bout Frenchy," Captain John said. "He's a tough little man."

"I just hope nothing happens to him."

"Frenchy is more capable of taking care of himself than any of those other men are."

"But he's just a boy!"

"The likes of which you may never see again. He knows this river and the sloughs and the land around them better than anyone. He was taught by his Indian family."

"Indian? But he speaks French."

"He was raised in a rich French culture by his father, a French trader. But his mother was Winnebago, and his Indian cousins taught him to fish and hunt, but I don't think he's ever been to any school."

"His father never sent him to school? Must not be much love there."

"On the contrary," the captain said. "You've seen Frenchy's fine wooden canoe?"

"Yes."

"Well, his father brought that to him from Montreal... crafted by one of the best French boat swains... probably cost him a fortune."

"It *is* a fine canoe. But he seems to be very smart. Why hasn't he gone to school?"

"Don't know. You should ask him next time you see him."

12.

Frenchy convinced the sheriff that he should first scout the backwater channel alone, as he in his sleek canoe could maneuver more quietly. The sheriff, however, insisted that he take at least one armed deputy with him. Jack Hensley was selected. With the Wenona sitting well back from the mouth of the slough, they slipped the canoe into the water; Frenchy and Hensley set out on their mission.

A column of grayish-blue smoke spiraled up among the trees and dispersed into the breeze. There was a campfire, meaning someone was on the island, but there was no sign of the steamboat that Frenchy had seen there before. He landed his canoe in the same spot, and with bow at the ready, Frenchy stole silently through the underbrush across the flat island to where he had a clear view of four men sitting on wooden boxes situated around the campfire. They seemed to have little concern for their surroundings as they ate beans from tin plates. Their hideout camp was relatively safe; isolated from the Wisconsin shore line with several swampy islands between them and solid ground, and well hidden from the main channel of the river, it was unlikely that anyone—even hunters—would chance upon them. And they would certainly hear oars of any approaching rowboats.

Beyond them, at the edge of the backwater lagoon laid the moored barge, in which was stacked all of Peter's goods. Now that he knew some of the bandits were there, Frenchy backtracked to Jack Hensley waiting at the canoe. He whispered to Jack, "There are four men there now guarding the barge with Peter's goods, but the steam bateau is gone."

"I'm going over there to take a look," Jack said.

"No, M'sieur Jack... they might hear you. We should go back to the Wenona and get the others."

"They didn't hear you," Jack argued. "They won't hear me either."

"But I am quieter on my feet," Frenchy warned.

"See here, kid... I'm gonna take a look and you're not goanna stop me."

"I won't stop you," Frenchy said. "But their guns might."

Jack pushed his way past Frenchy and started toward the pirate camp, disregarding the boy's warning. Frenchy just watched. He desperately wanted to paddle his canoe back to the Wenona and alert the sheriff of the situation, but he didn't want to leave Jack there alone. Somehow he knew that Jack was leading himself into trouble.

A few minutes passed; as far away as Jack had moved, Frenchy could still hear his booted footfalls, snapping twigs and disturbing rocks, his body sweeping through the foliage. Certainly, the pirates would hear him, too. And then Frenchy heard the raised, alarmed voices. The men in the camp had noticed Jack's approach. After witnessing their brutal, barbaric actions on the Little Frank, Frenchy was sure they would not let even an innocent hunter discover their camp, or allow him to escape alive.

The first two gunshots sounded from the camp; Frenchy was sure the next two were return fire from Jack's Colt .44 revolver. He quickly checked his quiver, and then, like a rabbit chased by hounds, he swiftly and quietly dashed toward the camp, but far to the left of Jack's position. If the pirates were shooting at Jack and focusing their attention in his direction, Frenchy thought he might have the advantage to get closer without being noticed.

Just as he suspected, the four men had positioned themselves behind trees for protection from Jack's bullets. He had come up on their flank and easily remaining concealed in the underbrush, he nocked a deadly hunting arrow, took careful aim—not to kill, but to render his target less harmful. The arrow flew silently just as Jack's .44 barked thunderously, echoing among the woods as if ten guns had been fired. But unlike Jack's slug, Frenchy's arrow found its mark in the first pirate's right leg. He yelled out in agonizing pain and toppled over. The other three men apparently assumed he had been hit by Jack's fire and didn't notice the arrow, or the direction from where it came, and continued the barrage on Jack.

The volley of gunfire had been heard at the Wenona, too. Some of the posse members had already launched their skiffs and were waiting at the mouth of the slough. When the first shots sounded they immediately began rowing into the backwaters.

Now it seemed obvious that a surprise attack in force was no longer a useful ploy; the sheriff ordered the Wenona pilot to navigate his boat toward the battleground, as creating detectable noise was no longer an issue. The pilot signaled the engineer and they were underway. The Wenona soon caught and overtook the men in the rowboats; they clung to the gunwales and were towed along until they came to Frenchy's canoe. There they let go, grounded the skiffs, and continued on foot toward the sound of the gunfire, greatly diminished now from when it began.

There was no sign of Frenchy or Jack Hensley, but they could plainly hear Jack's .44. Stray lead was still flying, slowing their progress to the side of the island with the pirate camp. But the shots seemed to be from only one firearm within the camp, in opposition to Jack's Colt .44. The posse men advanced carefully, crawling mostly to the vicinity of Jack Hensley. When they finally reached him, they found that he had been hit twice—once in the leg, and once in his right arm. He had continued to return the enemy fire with his left hand.

Then the gunfire from the camp ceased with a blood-chilling scream, followed by despondent moans of pain.

"There was four of 'em," Jack told the others. "But I think I got
199

'em all."

Indeed there were no more gunshots. The island lay silent in a bluish haze of gun powder smoke as the Wenona edged up to the bank near the barge. Only the pilot from his elevated view saw the true picture of what had happened; the four men of the camp lay on the ground, bleeding from their wounds as the six deputies who had remained with the boat rushed ashore, rifles and revolvers trained on the wounded outlaws, ready for any desperate last actions.

"These men have been shot with arrows!" one of the deputies announced, and then he called out to the sheriff who was with the posse in the woods, "They're all wounded and disarmed! Come on in."

The sheriff came into the camp after dispatching two of the posse assisting Hensley to the steamboat. He inspected the four outlaws, arrows piercing arms, legs, and shoulders. "Who did this?" he asked.

"I did, M'sieur," came the answer from Frenchy as he emerged from the underbrush, his bow still at the ready to launch an arrow.

"You aren't a very good shot, are you? All you did was wound their arms and legs."

"But, M'sieur... that's where I was aiming. I do not wish to kill any man. I only kill animals when I need to eat."

"I see... and where's this boat that you said you saw here?"

"It was gone when we came."

The sheriff turned to the first wounded man. With certain angry authority in his voice, he spoke. "We'll get you to a doctor, but where's the boat and who's on it?"

The man just stared at the ground, mute, and clutched his arrow-pierced leg.

Then the sheriff grabbed the pirate's shirt collar and roughly hoisted him up. "I asked you where is the boat? Who's on it?"

In a Spanish sounding voice the man finally answered as he glared at the sheriff with black, cynical eyes, "I do not know where the boat is now, but you will never catch Señor Bell."

"Bell!" said the sheriff. "Just as I thought. Were you with him last night on the raid of Little Frank?"

"No, Señor. We were here in our camp. We do not travel with Señor Bell."

The sheriff turned to Frenchy. "Did you see these men on Little Frank last night during the raid?"

Frenchy studied each of the four men. "No, M'sieur Sheriff. These men were not there."

"Are those goods in the barge what you were guarding on the La Crosse levee?"

Frenchy walked a few steps to the barge and examined its contents just to be sure. "Oui, M'sieur. These are Peter Story's goods."

The four men were officially arrested and taken aboard the Wenona while the boat crew lashed the barge to the steamer. When everyone was aboard, the Wenona and barge moved through the canal from the lagoon, out to the main channel, and then steamed upriver toward Brownsville.

"Who is *Señor Bell?*" Frenchy asked the sheriff.

"You're too young to remember, perhaps," the sheriff explained. "A few years back, Dr. Bell's pirate gang struck this area… attacked and robbed a cargo boat on its way to McGregor, Iowa. But they killed the boat captain. A posse from McGregor finally caught up with them at an island near Wyalusing the next day. They had recovered the stolen freight from the raid, but Bell managed to slip away in the fog after a gunfight, and he was never seen again."

"Will you go after Bell, M'sieur?" Frenchy asked.

"No… he has too much of a head start. We'd never catch up to him. Perhaps the next time he strikes, he won't be so lucky."

13.

The four prisoners were taken to the hotel at Brownsville where Dr. Riley attended to their wounds, and they remained under heavy guard. They would be moved to the La Crosse jail later that night.

Peter was located at the village restaurant. He was quite pleased to hear that his entire inventory—minus a few cans of beans—had been recovered. "You can thank that French speaking Indian boy," the sheriff told him. "If it hadn't been for him, we would never have found their camp."

"Yes, I am quite grateful to him. But how did those pirates know to strike the Little Frank... on that particular night?" Peter asked.

"We don't know that," the sheriff replied. "Maybe we'll never know."

"May I get my goods loaded on the train now?"

The sheriff pulled out his pocket watch. "It'll be too late today," he said. "The afternoon train will leave by the time the Wenona can get that barge up to Grand Crossing. But I'll have a deputy stand guard with it until it gets loaded on the morning train."

"Thank you Sheriff. Is the French boy still at the landing?"

"He is, and he's waiting for you."

"That's good. He'll be my guest at the Western Enterprise Hotel tonight... for a hot bath, a luxurious meal, and a comfortable bed. He deserves nothing but the best."

Peter sent Frenchy on his way the next morning with a Gold Eagle in his pocket and a big smile on his face. "I'll see you next time," he told the boy.

"Oui, mon ami," the boy replied. "Next time."

As the ferryboat steamed away from the La Crosse levee, Peter's gaze from the main deck noticed the moored Little Frank.

It looked so lonely and abandoned. He sincerely hoped that Captain Foster and his crew were all well, and that he would soon see them again. They were certainly lucky to be alive, and they were lucky to have such a good friend in Frenchy.

Frenchy. How could Peter ever repay the boy for his heroic deed? Perhaps on his next trip to La Crosse he would bring the boy a fine present; or perhaps he would offer Frenchy a job at his store, for he would need more help when he expanded and his father completed the new hardware and lumber business. Peter filled his lungs with the river valley air. It was going to be a great day.

At the railhead, Peter once again found the freight master. "My goods are in a boxcar?"

"Yes," the railroad man replied. "Your cargo is safely loaded."

"And did Sam, the conductor, get word of the delay to my father?"

The freight master frowned. "Mr. Story... did you not hear?"

"Hear what?"

"Sam will never work for this railroad again. He was shot in the shoulder with an arrow while fraternizing with pirates..."

BIGGER
ROCKS

BIGGER ROCKS

J.L. Fredrick

Does history repeat? The jury is still out. Some say it does. Some not. There are as many opinions as there are jurors.

I have a theory about repeated history, but before I dive headlong into it, let's look at some of the basics first.

We can define history as a recorded chronological chain of significant events that have already occurred, or simply, a story of the past. There are two key words here: events, and past. Events are occurrences, incidents or experiences, especially those of some significance; past means not of the present.

Examining these words more closely we can safely say that any time, whether it is five minutes ago, yesterday, or a thousand years behind us is definitely the past. No gray area there. The past is the past. Cut and dried. Event, though, requires a certain degree of consideration when associated with history. Events occur by the millions every second of every day, but they are not necessarily history. Example: you discover a fly backstroking in your *Kool-Ade*. An event? Certainly. Significant? Only to you because you don't want to include insects in your daily diet.

History? Only to the fly.

Events can be classified in two categories: (1) natural occurrences such as storms, earthquakes, volcanic eruptions – the atmospheric and geological conditions over which we have no control; (2) created occurrences – those events that would not have otherwise happened without a push from man – wars, inventions, exploration, and so on.

Are you with me so far? Good.

Now let's consider the two main elements that qualify an event to be historically significant. (1) Did the event cause a condition that shaped the course of our existence? (2) Was it significantly noticed?

There can (and do) exist some contradictions to the formula when we consider examples of events. In a world so complex, we are surrounded by rules and their exceptions, theories and speculations. Man has not yet unleashed the power to gaze into a crystal ball and determine – without a doubt – the outcome of an event had it taken an alternate path. All we can do is theorize and speculate.

A tree fell in the forest of Montana 400 years ago. Historically significant? Hardly. Not until man comes along, finds the petrified remains and decides he needs to know why the tree fell and how old it was at the time. Now that fallen tree has become significantly historical – at least to that guy in the white lab coat. But did it make a difference in the course of our everyday lives? Not really.

A volcano erupted on an uninhabited island thousands of miles at sea. The island's formation was drastically altered; all vegetation destroyed; earthbound creatures perished at the will of hot lava and fire and smothering ash. Those that survived probably drown trying to escape. Birds soared off in search of survival on another coast. The island died, becoming nothing more than a glob of barren lava rock battered by the ocean surf.

Historically significant? To some – yes. Was it noticed? By some – yes. But did it change our lives? No.

We can come up with thousands of examples like this that contradict our values of events in history. The degree to which each one affects us personally determines the amount of significance we assign to the event. It's difficult for anyone to realize the significance of an event that occurred a millennium ago, after it has been diluted and laundered by time.

So let's consider some similar events that happened more recently and that had an express affect on mankind. We can all relate more readily to incidents involving natural disaster if they occurred within our lifetime, or within the lifetime of our most recent ancestors; such events probably levied an affect on our lives in some way.

Nearly everyone can recall the devastating earthquake that shook San Francisco from it foundations in the middle of the 1989 World Series, and are reminded of a similar occurrence in that city in 1906. When Washington State's Mount Ste. Helens blew her top in the '80s the whole country took notice, and for those living there and in neighboring states life was, at best, miserable. People of the Mississippi River Valley suffered the agony of losing everything they had to the silent deadliness of uncontrollable floodwaters in the 1920s and again in the 1990s. Throughout our nation's history residents of Florida, Louisiana, Texas and the entire Eastern seaboard have been driven from their homes by relentless hurricanes – so significant that we gave those storms first names. Forest fires deliver their infernal wrath on the hills of California, Montana and Wisconsin; lethal tornados strike and level entire cities across the land.

The gruesome facts remain: hundreds of lives were snuffed out; billions of dollars worth of property was lost; indelible memories were etched in the minds of thousands of people who endured those calamities.

Historically significant? Without the slightest doubt.

Now flip the coin over. Take a look at the other event category I mentioned earlier: created events. These are the events that are triggered by the hand of man. They are so widely varied in terms of complexity and result; it would take volumes to discuss even a minute fraction of the broad-range effects they have delivered to our doorsteps. But we can examine this category in a general sense keeping in mind three simple words: good, bad, and ugly.

All through time, man has faced struggle in some shape or form. (Bad.) From the earliest symbols and unpretentious pictures primitively scratched on a cave wall, we know that man learned to hunt and to gather his food to survive. (Good.) As his intelligence amplified he learned to store quantities of that food to help preserve his existence through lean times, or maybe he did it because he didn't want to spend all his time hunting and gathering. (Perhaps on a hot summer day he'd rather lounge on the beach or take the wife and kids for a Sunday ride on the family brontosaurus.)

Then his number grew. The population exploded and that's when things started turning ugly. He had to devise ways to protect his territory so the competition wouldn't deplete the food supply within his own little kingdom, forcing him to rack up unnecessary miles on the brontosaurus in search of sustenance elsewhere. A need for power over his neighbors in the duplex cave on the other side of the mountain created an urge to develop weapons of defense, and he immediately plotted boundaries for his adversaries to honor.

This all would have worked out okay – except for one little problem: the neighbors in the duplex cave on the other side of the mountain were developing and plotting as well, but they were one step ahead. They had covertly spied on the neighbors from the top of the mountain, returned to their duplex cave, attached bigger rocks to the ends of their clubs and set out to establish boundaries infringing on the party of the first part. Not only did they create more effective weapons; they acquired a faster brontosaurus too.

Well, now you can see how the art of war got started. Every

little kingdom, from the beginning learned posthaste the advantage of possessing the biggest rocks and the fastest brontosaurus. It might also be added that from these early stages of development the birth of ingenuity, invention and exploration eked their way into man's repertoire of abilities. If he didn't have the resources to develop the contraption to throw even bigger rocks at his opponent, staying safely out of range of the one at the end of a swinging club, he packed up his arsenal of smaller rocks, loaded them on his slower brontosaurus and departed for new, unknown territory. Thus, the enemy with the biggest rocks gained control of a larger kingdom while his departed neighbors explored, in search of new diggings.

This just about sums up the beginning of man's quest of domination. The power to control a larger domain has remained the priority of nearly every civilization since. The Romans wanted to conquer the world; Hitler wanted to reign over his perfect race; Saddam Hussein wanted to control global energy, and the list goes endlessly on. But with every offensive action comes rebellion: the Colonists rebelled against unfair taxation; humanitarians rebelled against slavery; the Hatfields rivaled the McCoys. (And nobody remembers why!) Anyway, you get the picture. In all walks of life there is always someone wanting a bigger slice of the pie; whether it be a madman with an army and scud missiles attempting to control the world, or the neighborhood thug with a switchblade wanting to relieve you of the possessions in your purse, the scenario is basically the same: the quest for domination.

No one can predict – even in retrospect – what the outcome would have been had General Lee not surrendered at Appomattox in 1865. We can speculate. The Civil War between the States probably would have ended soon anyway – because General Grant had bigger rocks.

And what would have happened if the World Wars had ended differently? If Germany had not signed an armistice in 1918? If the atomic bomb had not been perfected until after

1945? We can speculate. The weaker forces in both conflicts would have eventually been defeated anyway because great men like Pershing, MacArthur, Eisenhower, Mitchell and Patton maintained the bigger rocks.

Wartime events have continually marred the face of progress. Not a single person in today's society is unaffected by the results of war.

Obviously, there is a lot more to history than war. There is a definite bright side to consider as well. Man has always sought ways to make his life easier, more comfortable, and more productive. It hasn't changed from the beginning and it's not likely to change in the future.

Backtrack with me now to our friend in the duplex cave. His name is Oog.

When Oog discovered fire, it was a phenomenon far beyond his comprehension. He didn't understand the scientific concept whatsoever, nor did he imagine then the future possibilities of this newfound discovery that he had accidentally stumbled upon. But he did know that fire produced heat and light, and that it kept his dark, cold duplex cave warm and bright on a chilly winter day. Oog knew he had something there.

It didn't take him long to figure out that his fire needed fuel to stay alive. After considerable trial and error with various substances, (I don't use the word experimentation – that word implies documenting facts and figures; Oog's penmanship was pretty lousy and he hadn't learned too much math yet.) He discovered that some materials would burn and keep his fire hot and bright; some would not. He finally determined that wood seemed to do the job, and dead, dry wood worked the best.

Well, once his supply of dry wood from the immediate surroundings was up in smoke, Oog was forced to gather it from outlying areas, and eventually that meant on the other side of the river. He learned quickly that the wood floated easily across the river, but he also found that wet wood doesn't burn too well. He had to find a means of getting the wood across the river while keeping it dry too. So... he invented the boat.

Now Oog had the means to transport the wood across the river, and even in adequate quantities, but it was back breaking work to get it from the riverbank to his cave and it consumed a lot of his time. It didn't allow him any leisure or time for hunting trips with the boys.

Oog thought, "Uga kaga gaga baga," which is cave talk for "There must be a better way." (Yes, Oog had evolved from just a being to a thinking being.) It took a generation, or so, but finally, somewhere along the line there was an Oog Jr. who invented the wheel.

So began the era of invention.

Sound a little silly to you? Well, it might not have happened exactly that way, but at least this illustrates how man evolved into the age of invention, and you can imagine how he eventually adapted his thought process to combining single tools, forming complex machines to help him accomplish his tasks more efficiently. This process never stopped. It became another of man's obsessions – to invent – in order to improve his lifestyle. We can be grateful that Oog Jr. got the wheels rolling; just think of where it has taken us. With the adaptation of that and other simple inventions, combining them, improving them, our society soon became dependent on them and couldn't survive without them. Take a look around you and try to imagine your life without all those gadgets, without all those appliances, without your family car, without glass on your windows, (without windows!) without nylon, Teflon, or silicone – the list could take forever to complete. You'd probably be uttering "Uga kaga gaga baga."

On that day in 1903 in Kitty Hawk, North Carolina, when Wilbur Wright made the first sustained manned flight, staying aloft for 59 seconds and covering a distance of 852 feet in a plane, Flyer 1 that he and his brother, Orville built in their bicycle shop, neither of them could even imagine jet aircraft soaring across the country and around the globe. In 1927 when Charles Lindbergh flew the Spirit of St. Louis across the Atlantic Ocean non-stop, it was still an unthinkable feat to land a man on the moon and bring him back again. But now we rarely gasp at the thought of sending men and women into outer space.

When John Stevens invented the steam-powered boat in 1802, little did he realize that Robert Fulton, nine years later would be the first to build and successfully navigate the Mississippi River with the SS New Orleans, a bigger, improved version of the travel mode that became a mainstay for the next century.

"Mr. Watson, come here. I want you," were the first words transmitted by Alexander Graham Bell over a telephone wire into the next room. The year was 1876. Today, the telephone is a way of life.

All these figures of our historical past were driven by the human nature – one of man's obsessions – to invent.

Another of man's tendencies that has driven him to greatness is his curious nature – his desire to discover, which differs from that of invention. Inventions usually are the result of discovery.

But discovery doesn't always involve invention, and it too envelops a wide variety of events. When man discovered fire and how to control it and to put it to use he didn't have to invent it – it was already there – he just discovered its usefulness. He didn't have to invent the fuel to keep it burning – the material was already there – he just discovered which ones worked the best.

Oog's neighbor, who decided he didn't want to put up with the demanding rigors of defense when he should have been hunting food for his family, ventured off into the unknown to find new hunting grounds. History shows us that he and others just like him must have traveled great distances; there is profound evidence that whole tribes or colonies migrated to different parts of the world, taking with them their cultures and languages, eventually developing new ones. By the thirteenth century this had become common practice, and some peoples were obsessed with discovering not only what lay on the other side of the mountain, but had expanded their quest to include the far reaches of the entire globe: what is at the end of that ocean?

So continued the desire to discover, and when man found the shores of new continents he didn't stop there. His exploration took him deep into those new lands, and although he didn't always realize exactly where he was, he gradually developed the technology (as primitive as it may have been) to determine direction and distance. Out of necessity man discovered new ways to survive. He discovered new methods of building shelter with the materials at hand and the new flora and fauna provided him new resources.

When Captain Meriwether Lewis and Lieutenant William Clark, commissioned by President Thomas Jefferson in 1803 set out on their journey up the Mississippi and Missouri Rivers to discover the Northwest Passage, before them lay a vast and uncharted land; their ultimate goal of exploration resulted in opening up a whole new world into which others after them followed and discovered even more new territories. Within a short period of time (short in terms of man's total length of existence) very little of western America had not felt the footsteps of modern man and his influential power of development. Cities were born, the railroad stretched its shiny rails into the frontier and soon our entire country was linked together as one big workplace and playground.

In 1752 Benjamin Franklin performed his famous kite and key experiment, discovering that lightning is a form of electricity. Like fire, electricity had been a part of our universe since there existed an atmosphere, but it took a man driven by curiosity to discover its scientific concept. By just a little over a century later, 1879, the problems with harnessing and mass generation of electricity had been solved, Thomas Alva Edison invented the electric light bulb, and by 1882 most of New York City streets were brightened through the night by electricity. It's too bad that Mrs. O'Leary didn't yet have a light switch in her barn in 1871 when her cow kicked over the oil lamp kindling the fire that destroyed a major portion of Chicago.

It is relatively easy to conclude that history – historical events – is largely the makings of man. But you may ask: What of all those natural occurrences – hurricanes, volcanoes, floods – that man had no part of creating? Aren't they significant events that affected our way of life?

Yes. They certainly are. But let's look at them in a different perspective. Was it the event itself, the earthquake, the storm, the forest fire, that was most significant? Or was it man's reaction to them?

We as a people have survived all sorts of catastrophes, both natural and created. We have survived wars as well as droughts. We have survived threats to our health in the form of widespread epidemics as well as attacks on our safety and freedom by terrorists – many, many times. We have conquered monumental problems, both natural and created. We have reacted. We have invented. We have explored. We have discovered. We have survived and we have grown.

It was man's reactions to all those natural disasters that were really more significant than the disaster itself. In the aftermath of any calamity in history, the affected people and their brethren bravely continued on, time and time again, rebuilding, restoring their lives, their communities, their hopes and dreams. And though it may have come at great cost to many, those events – natural or created – strengthened our integrity as a people and as a nation.

So? Does history really repeat? Are we caught in a continuum of time that circumvents us and replays certain scenarios over and over?

Wars start – all with a common cause: the struggle for power and domination. Wars end – with similar results: the guy with the biggest rocks wins.

Man continues to discover. He has battled the Black Plague and was victorious, as he is battling AIDS and will someday overcome. He has found the cure for Polio, as he will eventually find the cure for Cancer.

Man continues to explore. Courageous and curious he tread on strange lands. As technology progressed and ability expanded he walked on the moon.

Man continues to invent. Oog Jr. gave us the wheel; Thomas Edison gave us the light bulb; the Wright Brothers gave us wings; John Mauchly gave us the first electronic computer.

And now we arrive at the threshold of my theory to answer the question: Does history repeat?

Since I have professed that man is primarily responsible for significant events – either by action or reaction – and similar events do occur – with similar causes and results – I have but one conclusion.

Our Supreme Being created, in the beginning, just so many souls to occupy the bodies of just so many inhabitants on His earth. In time, there weren't enough souls to go around, so He had to use some of them over when the original body perished. The curious, the inventive, the dominating; the good, the bad, the ugly; their souls kept coming back to start wars, to discover more rings around Saturn and to invent better mouse traps. The good and the evil keep on repeating their old deeds and tricks.

With what better mind to pair up Sir Isaac Newton's soul than Albert Einstein? Perhaps Christopher Columbus was recycled into John Glenn. Colin Powell may have been Napoleon Bonaparte in a former life. Maybe Osama bin Laden carried around Adolf's old soul. Did Shakespeare return in Hemmingway?

What was that you said, Mr. Nixon? Et tu Brutus?

ABOUT THE AUTHOR

Born into a farm family in the late 1940s, J.L. Fredrick lived his youth in rural Western Wisconsin, a modest but comfortable life not far from the Mississippi River. His father was a farmer, and his mother, an elementary school teacher. He attended a one-room country school for his first seven years of education.

Wisconsin has been home all his life, with exception of a few years in Minnesota and Florida. After college in La Crosse, Wisconsin and a stint with Uncle Sam during the Viet Nam era, the next few years were unsettled as he explored and experimented with life's options. He entered into the transportation industry in 1975 where he remained until retirement in 2012.

Since 2001 he has twelve published novels to his credit, and one history volume, *Rivers, Roads, & Rails.* He was a featured author during Grand Excursion 2004.

J.L. Fredrick currently resides at Poynette, Wisconsin.

Made in the USA
San Bernardino, CA
20 March 2014